A NOVEL

DREAM WILD

D1714641

A NOVEL

DREAM WILD

ROCHELLE
POWELL

A Division of WINEPRESS PUBLISHING

Pleasant Word (a division of WinePress Publishing, PO Box 428, Enumclaw, WA 98022) functions only as book publisher. As such, the ultimate design, content, editorial accuracy, and views expressed or implied in this work are those of the author.

Unless otherwise noted, all Scriptures are taken from the Holy Bible, New International Version, Copyright © 1973, 1978, 1984 by the International Bible Society. Used by permission of Zondervan Publishing House. The "NIV" and "New International Version" trademarks are registered in the United States Patent and Trademark Office by International Bible Society.

Scripture references marked KJV are taken from the King James Version of the Bible.

Scripture references marked NASB are taken from the New American Standard Bible, © 1960, 1963, 1968, 1971, 1972, 1973, 1975, 1977 by The Lockman Foundation. Used by permission.

ISBN 13: 978-1-4141-0944-2
ISBN 10: 1-4141-0944-X
Library of Congress Catalog Card Number: 2007900175

TABLE OF CONTENTS

CHAPTER ONE

THE REQUEST

The handsome slender man tenderly kissed his wife goodnight. "Don't stay up too late," he whispered in her ear as he quietly left for the bedroom. Michelle watched her husband disappear behind their curtain door. Turning her gaze back to the dining room window she stood next to, she looked out at the snowy, moonlit trees. Her children were already tucked in for the night, soundly sleeping a few feet away in the living room. The quiet sound of their peaceful breathing reminded the mother of her own exhaustion.

Michelle was tempted to call it a night, but a wild thought was nudging her on. An adventurous daydream that started out as a spark earlier in the day was now blazing with intensity. If she gave in to exhaustion and went to bed she feared that her wild dream might fade in the light of a new day. When the sun was shining and her children were awake, there was no time for the mother to daydream or to even think straight. Michelle was convinced that her children did not sleep, they simply recharged, and during the day, her small cabin home resembled a giant pinball machine with three living and breathing bouncing balls. The Paulson pinball machine was quiet for now, giving the tired woman some much-needed time alone.

Busy children were not the only things that threatened Michelle's new idea. Her overactive imagination had already destroyed too many dreams before they were given a chance to become reality. It was always the same old story for her. Inside her small cozy home, she was safe and could dare to dream; outside, beyond the cabin walls, the world was a bit scarier for Michelle. Her "pet fears," the real live furry ones as well as the more creative imaginary ones, lived out there. They were once again laughing at her, taunting, daring her. Tonight, the wolf was the first pet fear to assault the vaults of her memory.

The Day of the Wolf had been a beautiful day. After bundling up her three-year-old daughter and two-year-old twin boys, Michelle nervously let them out to play. There had been a severe cold snap, when it wasn't fit for man or animal to be outside. It was the kids' first day out in weeks. Shayla, pretending to be a sled dog, pulled her fraternal twin brothers, Caden and Levi, down the driveway in her pink sled.

Mother stood at the kitchen window doing dishes with hawk-like eyes watching the youngsters. The boys had not yet learned the importance of keeping their hats, boots, and mittens on. Michelle kept a constant vigilance, watching for cold appendages. As the little "sled dog" pulled her precious cargo further down the driveway, the watchful mother gasped, dropped a plate into the sudsy water, and ran outside screaming.

A skinny wolf was headed right for the unsuspecting children! Shayla, hearing her mother scream, looked up and saw the hungry wolf approaching. Michelle reached the children, gathered them in her arms, and rushed them safely inside the cabin. The verse, Psalm 74:19, went through her mind like wildfire: "Oh, do not deliver the life of your turtle dove to the wild beast." That had been too close for comfort; she had to be on her guard for the wolves and cougars that lived in their woods.

Shayla's brief glimpse of the dog-beast stalked her dreams for several weeks. She would wake up screaming from her nightmares, only to be comforted by Mom or Dad lying down beside her. Psalm 56:3 was repeated frequently to the little child: "What time I am afraid, I will trust in thee." Matters were not helped any by the fact that all of her blankets had pictures of wolves on them. Shayla's Grandma Barker loved giving the kids toys and blankets with a wildlife theme. It was probably a good reminder to the children that they lived in the woods. Michelle, knowing that Shayla did not currently need those reminders, folded the blankets up and put them out of sight.

A year before, Michelle was able to do a lot of cross-country skiing behind their place on the snow-mobile and dog sled trails. She enjoyed skiing with a passion and was disappointed that she had no one to share the passion with. Her Scandinavian husband had at one time loved the sport and had competed in many high school races. When they were dating, the two joyfully shared many ski outings. After getting married, Jerry's handyman business consumed all his energy and ambition. Michelle was left to ski by herself.

Before Shayla was in the picture, Michelle went out for hours at a time to explore new trails. Skiing was free—minus the initial cost of the equipment—and free was important. Money did not grow on trees in the Paulson household. Besides being free, Michelle's sense of adventure was satisfied when a new trail was discovered and thoroughly explored. She was always thrilled to tell Jerry of her new conquests, secretly hoping to arouse his old interest. Skiing was how Michelle feasted on the fresh brisk winter air. It kept her in some semblance of shape over the long winter. The rush it gave her was a living reminder of her earlier marathon running days.

What Michelle enjoyed the most about skiing was the fact that she was outside. She loved being outdoors. When the weather was too blustery to be out and about, being inside her cabin wasn't all that bad; the windows were so large that she felt like she was outside anyway. The woods surrounded the cabin, and there was no yard to separate her from the trees or the trails. Michelle could sit on her front step, put on her ski boots, step into her skis, and immediately be on a ski trail heading off into the woods.

Michelle's love for skiing was cooled off by a rare and unexpected cougar attack. The cougar, which was believed to be an abandoned pet, took down a horse less than five miles away. The unfortunate event made the news and became the topic of many conversations, including Michelle's. She had not given much thought to cougars until then; now it consumed her. Michelle's skiing season came to an abrupt and early end. Different scriptures of courage presented themselves in her mind, but even those could not overcome her cougar fear. She begged Jerry, to no avail, to buy her a sidearm so she could continue to ski. Since the money tree was bare, she went without the gun.

To the outward appearance, one would not think her to be a scaredy cat. Michelle's five-foot, five-inch frame was sturdy and more muscular than fat. Her tomboyish manner and love of carpentry allowed her to work side by side with the strongest of guys framing in houses, garages, and cutting down trees. Michelle's thrifty husband once took her to a job splitting firewood. He neglected to tell her beforehand that she was the wood splitter. "It was only one cord of wood, I didn't figure we needed to rent a splitter for that," he replied to an icy stare. Michelle's appearance was strong and sturdy; she was very durable. As a youngster, Michelle bemoaned the fact that she did not resemble a Barbie doll; as an adult, she gave thanks that she was of a sturdier stock. Her tomboy passions demanded endurance.

As much as she loved skiing, she also loved building and had scars to prove it. In her teenage years, Michelle's left hand ring finger had been cut off in a high school shop accident. The table saw hit a knot in the board she was working with. The rest was a blur as she looked down at her numb hand with the dangling fingertip. She saw the blood and thought, *Maybe I should cry*. Thankfully, the surgeon's successful operation restored the finger to use. Within a couple months of the accident, she was back in the shop working with the table saw. It would take more than a cut-off finger to keep her from making sawdust.

To one who saw Michelle wearing her carpenter's belt and in action with her power tools, she gave the appearance of being one tough cookie. Inwardly, Michelle was not a toughie, nor was she very brave. She regretted the fright movies and scary books she exposed herself to as a teenager. Now as an adult she struggled to go to the outhouse at night. Her mind was flooded with images of a masked man carrying a chainsaw, cutting a death path toward her. Thoughts of a bloody doll with a butcher knife, and dead, crazed, pets resurrecting after being planted in the pet cemetery also haunted her. These images would be with her forever.

Michelle was thankful that she had received Christ as her Savior at the age of nineteen. She had grown quickly enough in the Lord to know better than to continue watching such things. Even though she was cautious, a few innocent movies, such as Jack London's *Call of the Wild*, slipped by. Jerry and Michelle watched this movie late one night and had enjoyed it. There were, however, a few fictitious scenes of wild wolves that ravenously ate people. The next day when Michelle strapped on her skis, she soon faced her fear.

The ski started out rather lightheartedly. Michelle was drinking in the brisk winter air and enjoying the beautiful sunny day. Everything went well until she started thinking about the movie. She knew it was ridiculous.

"Wolves don't usually eat people. They're more scared of us than we are of them," she said aloud to the growing monster inside of her head. As rationalism faded and her fear grew, she quoted the scripture: "God hath not given us the spirit of fear, but of power and of love and a sound mind." Her pace quickened, and her sound mind left on the same wind that brought to her the long eerie howl of dog-like creatures. The howl was clear and unmistakable—a pack was nearby.

Michelle's skis were suddenly turbo-charged. She had no idea she could ski so fast. *If I don't end up as wolf food, maybe I should enter a race*, she thought. She frantically kept the pace up, panting, and continuously looking over her shoulder. *If I'm devoured, I wonder if there will be any bones left for Jerry to find? How long would it take for Jerry to realize something was wrong?* She dismissed those thoughts and forced herself to slow down in preparation for the intersection. She had to be ready to turn right and get off the circle loop she was on.

She did not want to slow down; the wolves might be gaining. Surely they had picked up her scent and could smell her fear. Suddenly, she slowed down and came to a stop. She could not believe her eyes. Was this really true? Looking on the ground, she saw her ski tracks were covered up by the fresh markings of a dog team mushing the same route. A spontaneous smile and a chortled laugh broke out as she realized what was really following her. She gained her composure and headed home just a little bit slower.

Allowing her thoughts to return to the present, the weary mother turned her gaze from the window. Michelle would not let her pet fears paralyze her tonight. Her wildest dream was nudging her on. Her smile grew large as she thought of what she would do next. With her children in bed and her husband soundly asleep, she could now stay up and "Stephanize."

Stephanie Summer was the object of her thoughts tonight. Tenderly, Michelle picked up the e-mail machine and placed it on the table. She turned it on and began emailing her dearest friend.

Steph was about eight years younger than Michelle. They met at a Bible study Stephanie's father had taught. Michelle began attending the study when she was eighteen. Shortly thereafter she accepted the fact that she was a sinner bound for hell, unable to save herself by any good merits of her own. Only a personal acceptance of Jesus Christ's payment for her sins on the cross, His death, burial, and resurrection could atone for all her sin failures. As Michelle studied the Scriptures, growing in her walk with the Lord, her relationship with the young preteen, Stephanie, also grew. It blossomed into an incredible friendship, filled with adventure.

The beautiful, olive-skinned Italian brunette was a tomboy after Michelle's own heart. Despite Stephanie being a tomboy, Stephanie's mother, Dayna, did her best to raise a well-mannered young lady. Dayna was careful, however, not to squelch the sports fiend and adventure-driven spirit that resided in that olive skin. Michelle studied the young girl and her family, learning much about manners and proper etiquette from them, but when the two of them were alone, there wasn't anything Stephanie could not be talked into.

Dayna prayed hard for her daughter when the two friends were together and out of her sight. Those prayers were not without reason. When Stephanie came home after time spent with Michelle, she would tell her mother about their big adventures. Once, much to Dayna's dismay, Michelle had shown the young and impressionable Stephanie how to go "forking." Dressed in black and protected by the moonless night, the two friends left Michelle's house in her Plymouth minivan. Parking a block away from their target, creeping through the shadows, they paid a visit to their slumbering friends. When they were all done with their deed, their unsuspecting friend's yard looked like winter had hit. Hundreds of plastic forks had been stuck into the lawn and were accompanied by a thin layer of finely shredded toilet paper. The basswood tree showed off its nice white streamers of wiping material and was topped off by little Jimmy's mountain bike dangling from a branch.

Other adventures would begin innocently at church. While visiting with Stephanie after a Sunday evening service, Michelle was struck by the sudden urge to go camping—now. With a twinkle of mischief in her eyes, she asked the brunette if she was booked for the next day or so. She then proceeded to invite her camping. With the spark of adventure lighting in Stephanie's eyes, she smiled, disappeared, and then momentarily reappeared. She had the reluctant permission of her parents. At eight o'clock, the twosome left church, hit Steph's place to pack, then drove an hour to Michelle's. After arriving in Ely, Michelle packed her gear, loaded up the canoe, and drove to a neighboring lake. By the light of the moon, they paddled to an island and pitched a tent. The remainder of the night was spent talking and laughing. The next day found the two ladies exploring a new lake and some rapids.

Steph was Michelle's biking, hiking, skiing, canoeing, and camping partner. The two made a great team. When they weren't recreating together, they would go and visit people they both knew in hopes of leading them to Christ. Michelle was open and transparent with Steph, sharing hopes, dreams, goals, and failures to the point of embarrassment. Steph was more reserved, limiting her conversation to facts rather than feelings. On one occasion, Michelle told Steph, "I've come to the conclusion that you're not human."

"What!" gasped Steph.

"You heard me," replied the older. "I share my guts with you till there is nothing left inside. You've seen me cry, laugh, stomp, and snort—but you! You never show emotion. I've never seen a tear come out of those pretty brown eyes. You're always as cool as a snake. The only hint I have of your humanity is the occasional migraine you suffer from. A robot wouldn't have that problem."

Even though Stephanie's reserved nature often irritated the bubbly Michelle, it did have a calming affect on her. It made her a little less apt to share unimportant details, such as how she clipped her toenails or what she ate for breakfast that day. It kept Michelle in check.

"Dear Stephanie," the e-mail began as Michelle quit daydreaming and clicked her mind into typing mode. "You've been on my mind tonight, and I wanted to write and tell you one of the things that I like about you. I love your spirit of adventure. Even though marriages and miles separate us, I often reminisce on our adventures and covet more." At this point, Michelle's e-mail started getting a bit sappier than she really wanted. Michelle truly missed her friend and desired only to convey to Steph the dear value of that treasured friendship. Upon Michelle's request, Jerry would often proofread letters to Steph before they were sent off. Upon completion of the last e-mail, he had shaken his head at the sticky Stephanie letter and simply said, "I wouldn't mind hearing you talk that way to me sometimes." Michelle was trying to behave and started to proceed to the point of her letter.

"Steph, I'm feeling the full extent of cabin fever right now, and I need an adventure to plan, something to look forward too. Would you be able to go camping with me this summer? Please respond and let me know what you think. I'll be living next to my e-mail machine until I hear your reply. Love, your adventure-hungry friend, Michelle."

CHAPTER TWO

THE REPLY

Michelle would have starved to death had she truly camped out next to the e-mail machine. Stephanie's reply was slow in coming. Eventually it came, and Stephanie's letter was equally as enthusiastic as Michelle's request. She too looked forward to an adventure with her old friend. Being that it was February and the summer was still a ways off, Steph found it hard to pin down a date for the trip. She would not know her summer work schedule for at least two more months. She did say, however, that Michelle should go ahead and pick out a route into the BWCA, one that could be comfortably taken in a weekend. That was all Michelle needed to hear. Now her daydreaming could have an outlet: maps. As she looked for her BWCA maps, she told her husband that she was planning a women's camping trip for the summer.

"Oh, that's nice," was his reply. He thought she was joking.

"Steph is interested. I'm going to ask some other ladies from church too."

Jerry smiled as he glanced up from the newspaper. Michelle, seeing his disbelief, asked with a twinkle in her eyes, "Could you find a sidearm for me before then?"

"Sure, honey, anything you want," joked the six-foot, one-inch, sandy-haired man.

Michelle's blue eyes held her gaze on Jerry's equally blue eyes. She thought to herself, *You just wait, I may be a chicken, but I still love adventure.*

Michelle had not always been such a scaredy cat. She used to enjoy all sorts of adventures without even giving a thought to the "what ifs." After she got saved, she could no longer claim the innocence of being naive. The Bible taught her too well what was in the human heart and the danger that it possessed. A couple months after her first child was born, she held the tiny baby in her arms and cried out to God asking, "How can I raise this baby in such a wicked world?" She had been reeling from the recent news. Muslim terrorists had leveled New York City's Twin Towers. The suicidal terrorists hijacked planes, flying the aluminum crafts with all their passengers into the tall structures. Thousands of people were killed in a matter of minutes. The human heart is deceitful.

Michelle never used to worry about body failures either. Having recently spent four months on bed rest, two of which were in the hospital, Michelle learned firsthand how fragile the human body was. Michelle's second pregnancy with the twins had been a rough one. It took her nearly two years to gain back the strength and stamina the bed rest had robbed of her. Back pain, migraines, and chiropractic visits had become a common thing for her. If Michelle's neck or back went out, a migraine would follow. Only a visit to her dear chiropractor would provide the needed relief.

Things that went bump in the night topped Michelle's fear list. Bears, wolves, cougars, toads, bats, and rats were just a few of the creatures that kept her guessing as she lay in her tent. Frogs jumping onto the outside of the tent were easy to figure out. It was the twig-breaking sound she dreaded the most. That noise ranked right up there with the masked chainsaw man and the bloody little doll. As Michelle grew older and wiser, she learned of more things to be afraid of, thus adding them to her mental fear list.

Sunday finally came and so did the hour-long drive to church. Michelle absent-mindedly watched the scenery go by. Mentally, she was planning. The camping trip would have room for up to nine women. Rules that governed the Boundary Waters Canoe Area (BWCA) of northern Minnesota regulated the number of canoes to three and people to nine. If there were going to be more than nine people, another permit would be required. The second group would have to travel independently from the first.

The law made for less congestion on portages and at campsites. Even though Michelle did not have a date set for the trip, she would begin immediately to drum up a roster of interested women.

Michelle pored over many BWCA maps and had a few routes narrowed down. She was looking for a mild-to-easy route. One that could be tailored to fit wimpy women but with enough of a challenge to leave some sore muscles and make the ladies trust God for strength. The lakes could not be too big; one windy day, blowing whitecaps the wrong direction, could spell disaster. Whitecaps were challenging enough for experienced canoeists. A narrow river route would not have whitecaps.

The route had to include a couple portages as well. She wanted everyone to experience the rocky deer trails of a portage path. There was a dark cloud rolling over her plans: the weather. Would it be hot, rainy, cold, or tempestuous? She had been on wet, rainy trips before and they were miserable. Michelle had taken her father, brother, and sister on one of those tent-flooding trips. It was her family's first BWCA experience. They left the woods with a cold, damp and foul taste in their mouths. They never returned. Michelle did not want a repeat of that trip. She needed to have all the bases covered to ensure that the women would have a pleasant experience. A backup plan was coming into view. Michelle would have to talk to her friend, Carmen, before she could further entertain this thought.

Jerry could only put up with so much silence from his wife. He interrupted her day dreaming, "What are you thinking so intently on?"

"My camping trip."

"What camping trip?"

"The all-ladies trip I told you about."

"Oh. That trip," he replied with a snicker.

"I am going to get a feel today from some of the ladies at church to see if they would be interested in going." Jerry was silent. "I would really appreciate it if you would encourage me to do this. Since the birth of the boys, I've been wrapped up in diapers and bottles. I feel rather disconnected from the ladies. I need to reconnect. I don't do well as an island."

She could have said more, but her point was made. Jerry remembered Michelle's concern when they first talked about marriage and tying the knot. "I'm worried that you'll put me in a pumpkin shell and keep me there very well," she had said. He loved her too much to do that. He wanted her to do things she enjoyed.

Jerry knew that camping was in her blood. It was one of the things that made her tick. It excited her almost as much as skiing and building. Michelle and Jerry, before knowing each other, had mental lists of characteristics they wanted in a mate. Each included that the other would love camping and spending time in the BWCA.

The million or so acres of raw forestland that made up the BWCA excited Jerry as well. He had been enjoying this wilderness area ever since he was a little child accompanied by his parents and only brother, Chris. He thrilled to explore new areas. The thought of Michelle going camping and leaving him home with the three kids did not bother him. What did eat at him was the fact that she might go on a new route and explore without him. He was always careful to share his pleasures and first-time experiences with her. He loved including Michelle on any adventure he faced. He was always saddened when she could not go. Michelle, on the other hand, could not get enough adventure. She always told Jerry, after the fact, where she had been and what she had done. Jerry's displeasure always showed on his face. He knew he had to guard his facial features, otherwise he suspected his wife might simply clam up and quit telling him of her adventures. "Oh Lord," he silently prayed, "please help me to overcome this jealousy and to be genuinely happy for Michelle."

The kids, just awakened from a nap, were stirring in the backseat of the truck. The close quarters of the cab could get awful noisy when all three were conscious. Jerry adjusted the rearview mirror to see the kids. The three car seats, with their precious cargo all carefully strapped in, were rapidly coming to life. Sometimes, especially on long trips, Jerry regretted having sold their minivan. Shortly after the sale of the van, they found out that Michelle was expecting twins. For a truck, however, the extended cab Dodge Ram was spacious.

As the boys grew, so did Michelle's baby fever. With Michelle's desire to have another baby, Jerry often contemplated buying a different family vehicle. The truck was Michelle's pet; calling it Tucker, she named it and claimed it. She would not easily part with her truck. Jerry brought home several minivans from the local dealer for Michelle to test drive. She was visibly pained to be sitting in them so low to the ground. "I feel like I've been demoted in these little tin cans," she declared. She had eyes only for her powerful, ruby-red diesel truck. Jerry was disheartened by his wife's passion for Tucker. His old work truck was failing. He would soon need his wife's truck for work. Her truck was bought brand new with the intention of Michelle driving it until it was paid off, then he would claim it for his business. In the meantime, it had been outfitted with a snowplow. It was readily available for plowing when his old truck would suffer a breakdown, which was happening more frequently. Jerry, once visiting with his buddy, asked him as he looked at Tucker, "Is it sin for me to covet my own truck?"

They were now a mile from church, and he quit thinking about his vehicle dilemma as he focused on the reason for the trip. Neither Michelle nor Jerry wanted idols of camping or trucks to get in the way of this important worship service. It was to worship the God of all glory for which they had driven an hour.

Tucker pulled into the church parking lot and safely came to a stop. The little car seat prisoners were freed and escorted into church. Shayla's short sandy hair bobbed with each step she took. Michelle sighed as she examined her daughter's boy-like haircut. Oh, how she missed those beautiful long locks that Shayla bore only a week earlier.

The three year old decided to experiment with scissors unsupervised. Michelle, finishing up some outside chores, entered the cabin and found long locks of hair lying on the bedroom floor in front of the mirror. As mother went to find the owner of those abandoned locks, she guiltily thought, *A child left to himself, bringeth his mother to shame.* Shayla sat innocently at the table, examining books, when Michelle found her. A swift punishment was executed but not too harshly. Michelle was secretly thrilled for the little girl. As Mom fixed up the do, she knew the two of them would get along so much better. Not having to daily detangle and torture her daughter's head would be a treat. Mother would miss the long locks, but the short, carefree haircut would feel wonderful this summer.

Even with short hair, Shayla was still cute. Cute was something Michelle would never look like with short hair. Her husband was careful to remind her of that fact when she talked about a change. Michelle was destined to have long hair forever. The length did hide some of the big-boned facial features she inherited from her dad's side of the family, and for that she was thankful.

Shayla was reintroduced to her Sunday school class. When dropped off, Mother had to explain the haircut story to her inquisitive teacher. Daddy brought the twins to the nursery, checked their diapers, and saw that they were playing contentedly. He quietly slipped out to find Michelle waiting for him in the church foyer. They were running a bit late and therefore only able to find seating in the front pew.

A tall, slender woman arrayed in a modest, but striking, black dress approached the podium. Delancy Joy Nyland, with her fragile one hundred-ten-pound frame, belted out the soprano notes like no one else in church. Sometimes the notes were so high and powerful that Michelle felt like eyeing her watch crystal to see if it would shatter. She enjoyed Delancy's specials but always wondered how a delicate creature like her could produce such penetrating sounds.

Jerry stretched out his relaxed arm on the pew back. Michelle snuggled in close to enjoy the special music. Michelle forced herself to concentrate on the words and not to sneak glances at her watch. The solo was beautifully done.

After some congregational songs and one more special, Pastor Ford Mackie took the podium and presented the Word of God to his flock. The pastor of Grace Bible Church was not a charismatic fire-and-brimstone-type of preacher. He was of the Finnish descent and spoke to a mostly Finnish congregation. That said it all. The Finlanders of northern Minnesota's Iron Range were even-keeled and unemotional in public. Despite this shortcoming, Pastor Mackie was able to deliver powerful messages that pointed one to a sovereign and holy God. Anyone with a heart after God would walk away encouraged and exhorted. Hearts that were calloused and hard usually did not persist in coming out. They would lose interest when the Holy Spirit started intruding in sensitive areas.

After the sermon and one last congregational song, people started to visit. Michelle and Jerry retrieved the kids and mingled too. Michelle approached Delancy and thanked her for the special music but then proceeded right to the point. Michelle hated to waste words if she didn't have to. A person's time was precious and valuable. She did not want to be guilty of wasting it.

"DJ," Michelle said, using her friend's nickname, "would you be interested in going on an all-women's camping trip into the BWCA?"

Her slender friend replied with an immediate and enthusiastic, "When?"

"Sometime around the middle of the summer. It all depends on Stephanie Summer's work schedule. As soon as I know more I can set a date."

"I don't care when it is. Count me in, I'm going."

I hope the other ladies are this receptive, thought Michelle. DJ's first real night spent in a tent had been with Michelle. Last Labor Day weekend, DJ, with her husband, Brant, along with Jerry and Michelle, had packed up their camping gear and dropped off the kids at the babysitter's. The four escaped for some much-needed R and R. They had a fantastic time trying to fish, hiking to a waterfall, reading, eating, and just doing nothing. The property they stayed at was on a remote point with no electricity or indoor plumbing. It had an outdoor latrine in which to do your business. The latrine was a simple wooden box with a lid.

The one-room cedar log cabin was small, cozy, and perfect. Michelle and Jerry opted to sleep in a tent, giving the fairytale cabin to the Nylands. During the last night out, a storm swept in with a ferocious wind. Jerry wanted to sleep in the cabin with the Nylands. Michelle's throat closed at the thought of being trapped in a small room where she could not easily get up and walk around. Her back was in a great deal of pain, and she needed to be able to get up and stretch. If she stayed in the tent, she could easily retreat outside and not worry about waking anyone. Michelle talked DJ into tenting with her. The storm was fierce; the guys could not believe their wives would give up the comfort of a cabin for a wind-tossed piece of fabric. Michelle consumed a couple painkillers and the ladies stayed up till four o'clock, reading and visiting. They gave themselves a reason to stay up, rather than from fear of the storm. For the California-born-and-bred DJ, it was a real adventure. One that she hoped would not be her last.

Michelle excused herself from DJ and made her way to several other women. Much to her surprise, the younger mothers were as eager as DJ. They would not have to be asked twice to go on a trip without all their kids. It was a golden opportunity.

The older women that were asked were more practical. Michelle's dear forty-year-old friend, Joan, simply asked if there would be a toilet that flushed. MaryAnn wanted to know if there would be a shower. Both women declined the invitation.

Dina was recovering from the birth of her twins, Lisa and Luke. She would not be going anywhere without them. That was too bad for Michelle. Dina, as a teenager, had lived in the BWCA for a summer with her unemployed mother and younger brother. She was a real kindred spirit for Michelle. They had a lot in common; both were married to Jerrys, both had a set of twins close to the same age, and both had a passion for camping.

Some of the ladies on Michelle's recruiting list were not there. She would have to corner them at a later date. For now, the reality of the February snow-covered earth kept her plans in check.

CHAPTER THREE

THE WORKOUT

February and March disappeared, and so did the snow. By April, the woods were dry enough for phase one of Michelle's new workout plan: cutting trees. Michelle was bound and determined to get in shape for her upcoming BWCA trip. She tried unsuccessfully to use the neighbor's treadmill and found it extremely boring to exercise inside. She tried to go for walks, but Jerry's schedule was never consistent, and he could not be counted on during daylight hours to be home to watch the kids. Taking the kids on a forty-minute walk was out of the question, for they did not own a stroller big enough for the three kids. Michelle was tied to the home front and had to get creative if she wanted exercise. Her back was still very weak from the months of hospitalization she experienced two years earlier. It was time for a change.

Taking one last glimpse to see that the kids were safe, Michelle put on her glasses, ear protectors, adjusted the choke, and pulled the cord. The chainsaw rebelled, coughed, and sputtered, but eventually came to a loud roar. Michelle chose a tree that was a safe distance from the kids. She attacked the dying poplar with zeal. Michelle notched the tree in the direction it would best fall. With an almost wicked laugh, she sliced into the back of the crippled tree. "Fall, baby, fall," she chanted as it crashed toward the earth. Once the giant was slain, it was swiftly cut up into firewood. She carried each chunk out of the woods by hand. When the only evidence of the act was sawdust, she looked for her next victim.

Poplars were everywhere. The dangerous, unpredictable trees were slowly being eradicated, one by one. Some were small, while others were at least forty inches around. A few trees were easily felled onto the driveway and carted away by Tucker. Most chunks had to be walked great distances to the pile. Phase-one was progressing nicely. The forest was dry and bug-free. The fresh air was invigorating.

The kids cooperated well and stayed out of harm's way. They played nicely with each other in their play area. The Paulson playground consisted of a fourteen-foot trampoline with sides, Shayla's double-decker playhouse, a sand pile, and the boys' little playhouse. Shayla tended to be a bit bossy with her brothers, but she had enough sense in her to keep the boys entertained and away from Mom. When another tree was close to coming down,

Michelle would yell to warn the kids. Cutting trees was addictive; she never wanted to stop. There were always more trees to come down. Some days she could easily cut up ten trees, other days only four or five. The work progressed for a solid two weeks until Michelle let her guard down.

It was a windy day, and Michelle knew better than to cut down trees in such weather. There was, however, one tree she really wanted down. It was by the end of the driveway, leaning toward the road. The wind, Michelle hoped, would push the tree in the opposite direction of the road and land it on the driveway. At least that's what she was banking on. If the tree fell on the road, it could mean death to anyone who might happen by. She notched the tree so it could fall on the driveway and then proceeded to the other side of the tree. No one was coming on the road, so she made the last cut. Before she could pull the chainsaw out, the tree tilted backward and pinched the saw into the tree.

When the wind let up, the tree threatened to fall road-ward. Michelle froze, not knowing what to do. "Why did I insist on cutting down this tree? Oh, if only Jerry was here." For five minutes she stood by the road, not moving, just watching the tree. She struggled but could not free the saw. Had it come free, she could cut the tree down on the road when it was clear of traffic. A desperate prayer went upward. "Oh God, please don't let my folly cost anyone's life. Please help me know how to get this tree safely down."

She now knew what needed to be done. Running to the garage, leaving the tree in God's hand, she found a rope and an eight-foot fiberglass stepladder. Catching her breath at the base of the crippled tree, she carefully set up the ladder. Next, she climbed up and tied the rope as high as she could reach. She knew the tree should have been roped off before she cut it. Quickly descending while still holding the rope, Michelle stretched it away from the tree to a more stable spruce. With the rope tied tight, she hung on and threw all her weight onto the rope in a bouncing motion. When the tree bent in her direction, she released the rope to flee, but it was premature. The tree straightened. She grabbed the rope and tried again.

This time the tree leaned and hovered in Michelle's direction. She kept her grip steady. The poplar bent from her weight and headed earthward. Michelle got out of the way just in time to see broken branches flying past her head. With the tree safely down on the driveway, she muttered a huge thank you to God for His help. Still a little shaky from the adrenaline rush, she moved to pick up the chainsaw. She examined it and found it undamaged. She gave herself a minute to regroup her thoughts and then went to clean up her last tree. The reality of the situation and the seriousness of her foolish decision hit hard. The addiction was cured, at least for this year. It would be back again next year.

Phase two: The pile of cut wood was massive, but Michelle would not be intimidated. She topped off the gas, checked the oil, and fired up the splitter. Its stinky, gassy breath nearly choked her. She'd get used to it and soon would be wearing the aroma like a perfume. With one whiff, Jerry would know what she had been up to that day. The task ahead of her was daunting. Her back was still complaining from the huge chunks she had piled there. With a renewed sense of determination, she lifted the back-breaking pieces for the last time. The wood splitter easily humbled the big pieces into a manageable size. The split firewood would have all summer to season. It would be ready by winter to be fed into the insatiable woodstove. Wood was the cabin's only source of heat.

The main goal that pressed Michelle forward in splitting the wood was not for the warmth of it but instead for the bending, lifting, and stretching of it all. The menial chore was a superb weight-lifting exercise. Day after day the splitting and stacking went on. Sometimes Shayla would put on her little work gloves from Grandma Paulson, her mother's extra ear protectors, and work the hydraulic controls while Michelle handled the wood. When all was said and done, about ten cords of wood had been cut, split, and stacked. Michelle stepped back, admired the nicely stacked wall of wood, and walked away.

Phase-three: Michelle did not like lingering in the memory of accomplishments. She immediately pressed toward the next goal. She had to keep moving. Her trip would be sneaking up on her soon. It was now mid-May. When she wasn't changing diapers, making meals, washing crayon off of wall and furniture, hauling water from the well, or running errands, her exercise program consumed what was left of her day. The phase-three workout meant making more sawdust.

Michelle should have been a furry rodent with a large tail and big front teeth. If there was a project at home that required the creation of sawdust, Jerry preferred to "Leave it to Beaver." Michelle did most of the construction and maintenance on the property, and she loved it. Jerry's long work schedule prevented him from doing much of anything at home. He was very helpful, though, when Michelle needed assistance. Michelle's honey-do list was always short to nonexistent; she usually ended up doing the task herself. If Jerry was asked to do something once and did not do it, she would not ask again.

The task now looming in front of her was to make siding for their sauna. A large pile of pine slab wood, recycled from a local sawmill, sat next to the garage. It needed to be peeled free of its bark. With a log peeler in hand, Michelle started her new abdominal workout. Peeling bark off of logs and slab wood was tiring work but well worth it. When the peeling was done, a circular saw was used to cut the two long sides. A grinder smoothed the surface of the wood and freed it from dirt and grime. After that, the siding was ready to be measured, cut to length, and vertically attached to the sauna. The finished affect was that of a log cabin. When Michelle had the sauna completely sided, she tore off the rotten deck and built a new one out of green treated lumber.

Michelle headed to the garage to grab a sander so she could finalize the project before lunch.

"Mommy," Shayla yelled from her playhouse. "When can we eat?"

Michelle, not wearing a watch, peered through the cabin window to see the clock. She sighed; it was ten after one. "I guess it's now; please round up the boys and come in." Michelle tried to keep lunch around noon, but sometimes her projects got the best of her. Every now and then, Michelle wished she was Jewish. At least that way, she would have to drop everything cold turkey to observe the Sabbath.

It was extremely difficult for Michelle to drop anything mid-project. Jerry, out of concern, would give little hints that his wife promptly ignored. He knew his wife was obsessed with projects. He was glad for all that she accomplished, but she could slow down. Her projects blinded her to things that were higher, nobler, and of eternal value. There were so many calls that needed to be made, children from Bible club that could be invited over, parents that could be followed up on, and lonely widows that could be visited. Someday he would talk with her about his concern, but first, he himself needed to slow down.

A simple peanut butter and jelly lunch was made and placed in front of the children. The blessing was said, and as the concluding "Amen" sounded forth the kids hungrily attacked the sandwiches. Michelle nibbled on hers and reached over to check the e-mail machine. Elation rocketed her spirit upward. Stephanie had finally responded to Michelle's most recent request for a camping date to be set. Michelle soaked up every word of the message. The smile on her face evaporated and her soaring spirit made a crash landing.

Stephanie was not able to go camping. Her schedule was booked. Her part-time job had turned into full-time summer employment. The remaining time off was quickly penciled in by a few weddings and two vacations with her husband.

The discouraged woman moaned, turned off the e-mail machine, stood from the table, and walked to the window. She looked out at nothing in particular. Stephanie's e-mail was a big blow. No one else on her roster of interested women had any real camping experience. From day one of planning and dreaming, Steph's presence had been visualized on the trip. Now Michelle had to readjust her thinking. Steph's face, strength, and encouragement had to be removed from the mental picture in Michelle's mind. The new picture looked dangerously wimpy and inexperienced.

Michelle realized she had, to an extent, elevated Steph to a position that only God should fill. In small ways, she was looking to her friend for happiness. Jeremiah 17:5 warned her: "Thus saith the LORD: cursed be the man that trusteth in man, and maketh flesh his arm, and whose heart departeth from the

LORD." Michelle did not want to dwell on this disappointment. Nor did she want to put her friend in the place of an idol. Instead, she brought the trip before God in prayer, trusting that God could be counted on to turn the heartbreak into encouragement.

CHAPTER FOUR

ANNIE

Sunday came quickly. After the conclusion of the morning service, Michelle walked straight into the church bookstore and removed a calendar from the white wall. She hurriedly found her timid friend, Annie. Cornering her before she could escape the church confines without notice, Michelle plopped the calendar in front of her and asked, "Would you be interested in going on a women's camping trip?"

A little smile could be seen on the corner of Annie Ojala's mouth. She meekly replied, "Yes."

"Well then, will you help me set a date for the trip?" Michelle wanted to find a weekend that would not conflict with Bible schools, camp, and the big Bruno wedding. She knew Annie had the summer off from nursing school and had a wide-open schedule.

"I don't know what days to pick, Michelle. Why don't you pick them?"

"OK then, how about the weekend of July 15, 16, and 17? Will that work for you?"

"I don't see why not."

"Good deal. If the dates don't work for other ladies, it might be a small trip with the two of us and possibly DJ. At least now we have some dates set and can better invite women."

Michelle sat in the church pew next to Annie, looking at the calendar. A huge smile engulfed her face. July 18 was her thirty-second birthday, and she was thrilled at the thought of having a camping trip to look forward to so close to that day. She would never call it her birthday party, but it would be a wonderful birthday gift from her husband to have three days all to herself without her beloved little shadows. If he happened to forget her big day, she would easily forgive him and thank him for his babysitting present to her. She knew Jerry would not forget. As long as he remembered to look that day at his "brain," her nickname for his palm pilot, he would see the flashing birthday cake telling him of the day's importance.

Michelle's mind wandered back to the present. Her eyes twinkled as she looked at Annie, then she remembered the calendar in her hand. She rose, walked back to the bookstore, and replaced the item on the wall with May on the front. She remembered a few other things she forgot to mention to Annie. When Michelle reappeared in the sanctuary, her shy friend had already vanished from the room. Michelle strode through the rest of the building, but there was no sign of Annie.

With a sigh, Michelle shook her head and chuckled. *Annie won't be able to disappear so easily on our camping trip,* she thought. *I can't wait to get better acquainted with her. It will be hard for her to disappear if she has to share a canoe with me. It could be a long swim back if she tries to leave.*

Michelle was very fond of the small, five-foot, one-inch woman. Annie's green and brown eyes lingered in Michelle's mind. She loved to see that shy lady break a smile. The expression on her face was usually very sober. Whenever a smile would penetrate, Annie's eyes shone and her face glowed. Her extremely curly, mid-length brown hair accentuated her rare smile.

Even though Annie was elusive, her quiet presence added value to any room or place she went. She was never boastful, was always kind and considerate, and was also a good listener. It seemed to Michelle that Annie's only goal in life, however, was to make herself invisible. It saddened Michelle to be unable to express to her timid friend what a treasure she was.

Annie had been coming out to church for over nine years and never caught on to the fact that people liked her and wanted to know her better. They wanted to be her friend. Michelle was one of those wannabes. She always looked for Annie at church, family camp, and other special church functions. One of Michelle's goals in life was to break the barrier that separated her from a possibly good friendship. It was a difficult challenge. Whenever Annie did make a rare appearance at a get-together, she always kept the visit brief and then disappeared. Getting Annie to answer the phone was just as hard. She screened her calls and rarely ever called anyone back.

A tough nut to crack, Michelle thought, *but it's worth every effort. I just hope I don't turn into a pest and frighten her off. She's just like one of those little chipping sparrows that visit our bird feeder by the dining room window. The poor creatures take to flight at the slightest movement inside the cabin.*

The disappointment of Stephanie's absence was fading a little as Michelle thought about this new challenge. "Dear Lord," she whispered, "help me to be a real friend to Annie." This prayer, she knew, would be uttered over and over as the trip approached.

Michelle glanced around the church foyer and spotted Annie's sister, Tami. She walked over to visit with her. Tami was thirty-three years old, about four years Annie's senior. The two sisters were total opposites. Tami, before her salvation, had been a loud and obnoxious gothic drug user. Her fingernails were always painted black, her clothes were all black, and her hair was purple. Her conversion caused a very morbid creature to die, and a new life resurrected in its place. Michelle always marveled at the new Tami. She would have been fearful to visit with the old Tami. She might have found a fist in her face had she offended the sordid lady. The new Tami was a real gem and easy to talk with.

Michelle was not going to talk about the camping trip with her. When it was first mentioned, Tami really wanted to come. She recently learned that she was pregnant. The awful morning sickness had been her first clue. When the sickness persisted, she had to quit her nursing home job. Had Tami only been pregnant and not sick, it still would not have been smart for her to go galloping off on a camping trip.

"Tami would have added a lot of flavor to the trip," Michelle mused. "Humph, I'd better enjoy this trip. Maybe next year I'll be the prego and unable to do another campout."

CHAPTER FIVE

THE PLAYHOUSE

On Monday morning, Michelle started phase four of her workout plan. Her playhouse/office/guest cabin—whatever she felt like calling it at the time—needed attention. *When this project is done,* she thought, *I've got to give this building a proper name and make a sign for it too.*

The little eight-foot-by-twelve-foot building she now faced was rich with history. It was borne out of a twelve-year-old's frustration. As a child, Michelle hated sharing a room with her brother and two sisters. She thought the world would end if she did not get her own space. She begged and pleaded with her carpenter pa to build her a playhouse. He was busy enough earning money to put food on the table and paying for electricity to keep the lights on. Her dad could not take on the project.

Michelle, being the stubborn Finlander she was, did not give up. She presented her sob story to a retired neighbor, who happened to be a carpenter. He took pity on the little gal and made her a proposition. Harvey Hartel offered to teach "Shelly," as he called her, to build a little house and to provide all the materials for it. She, however, would have to help him the whole summer, in his woodshop and abroad, on any project he might figure to take on. A deal was struck; an unlikely friendship began.

The crusty old pipe smoker remained true to his word and diligently taught his young friend many tricks of the trade. Shelly learned how to lay out skids, build a floor frame with joists on top, and to frame up stud walls. She learned about rafters, trusses, shingling, and much more. Her little playhouse blossomed and boasted electricity, carpeting, three sheetrocked walls, and one oak tongue-and-groove wall. The exterior was sided with T-111 and stained dark brown with white trim. The shingles were forest green. It was a miniature house. Harvey did not stop there; he made sure it had furniture. He showed Shelly how to build an entertainment cabinet, and together they built a glass-covered tongue-and groove-table.

It was a summer Michelle never forgot. She graduated from making rickety tree forts and now basked in the knowledge of building real little houses.

The playhouse was loaded onto Harvey's trailer and brought to the Barker property. Michelle's father helped to locate the new homestead not too far from the main house. A long extension cord reached the little house, giving it a life of its own, separate from the crowded Barker home. At first, Michelle spent much time in her little abode. However, Michelle soon grew tired of being by herself. As loneliness set in, the novelty of the little building wore off. Mr. Barker had also finished off three more bedrooms in the house. Michelle was quick to claim one. The playhouse was vacated and demoted to an interesting conversation piece.

The summer of Michelle's fourteenth birthday found her completing another eight-by-twelve building on the property. She saved all of her money, conned her mother into driving to Menard's, and came back with a vanload of materials to build herself a sauna. Her Finnish father eagerly bought a wood sauna stove and just as eagerly installed it for Michelle. He was very fond of saunas and soon had it broken in.

The sauna was to remain a permanent fixture of the Barker property. The playhouse, though, was relocated in 2001, six hours north to Ely, Minnesota. Michelle borrowed her father's trailer, loaded up the neglected structure, and hauled it to the Paulson homestead. Once situated in the great north woods, Michelle breathed new life into it. Being a huge eight months pregnant with her first child, Michelle slowly waddled around the little house and cosmetically touched up the interior. The playhouse was converted into a cozy guest cabin for the grandparents. They would be coming up in another month to meet their new grandchild.

The touchups would have stayed on the inside, but Jerry accidentally cut a balsam tree down in the wrong direction. It made a mess out of the playhouse roof and it had to be re-shingled. Michelle was all too eager to help. She moved slowly and cautiously, being very mindful of the edge of the roof. She had no intention of falling. After all the new black shingles were in place, Jerry told his wife she may want to keep the shingling project quiet until after the baby was born. He had seen his wife's caution, but he knew others would rebuke the woman.

The summer of 2003 found the little guest cabin being moved one last time. This time it was dragged by a come-a-long only two hundred feet further into the woods. Its new location nestled the structure nicely in a thick stand of balsam and spruce. The spot lent more privacy for company.

When Jerry jacked the guest cabin up to level it, a moment of carelessness cost him dearly. The jack handle flew out of his hand, cutting a permanent inch-long scar into his right cheek. Fortunately for Jerry, Michelle's friend, Krissy Riasanen, was up visiting. She put her nursing degree to use. Calmly, she assessed the situation and made Jerry lie down. She inspected the damage and began crafting homemade butterfly stitches out of band aids. She had him taped up and back on his feet in no time. Jerry did not do well with pain or blood. Seizures and fainting were his common reactions.

During Shayla's delivery, Jerry stole some of Michelle's nurses. He had worked himself into a seizure and lay helplessly on the floor. In between gasps of pain, Michelle simply told the doctors, "He's OK. He just had one of his seizures. You can put him on the recliner. He'll snap to after a while." It took a long while following the birth of their daughter for both bedridden parents to recover. Jerry would never be allowed to see another birth. Michelle did not like sharing her nurses.

Following the jack incident, the guest cabin was left alone for two years until the present. Michelle wanted to add on a little screened porch and new front steps. She also desired to install new siding. The cabin housed a bed, a small refrigerator, and a desk with Jerry's old computer on it. The building would multitask and also serve as a little office for Michelle to do her "think-tank" work.

Being eager to improve the value of their property, Jerry picked up some cedar plywood siding on sale. The "Beaver" went to work. Michelle attacked the project with enthusiasm. One by one, she carried the cedar plywood over from the garage. Measured for height, window openings, and the slope of the gable ends, the pieces were cut and ready to nail up. With her Stanley Bostitch air-nailer, the project went smoothly.

The wind drastically increased toward the end of the day. The last four-by-eight foot sheet of plywood was awkward to handle. A big gust pressed upon Michelle and grabbed the sheet from her grasp. As she struggled to regain control, the wind whipped the board again. Michelle felt something tear inside her shoulder. Then the burning sensation began. It was not an excruciating pain, but it grew terribly uncomfortable as suppertime approached. She managed to nail up the last piece but not without a struggle. She was careful not to move her shoulder any more than she had to. The tear considerably weakened her left arm. Certain positions were downright painful. Michelle decided to ignore her shoulder. She realized it probably just needed some time to heal. If it did not heal, a bad shoulder was not going to stop her from going on this trip. In case it did not heal, she felt it best not to mention anything about it to Jerry. He might overreact and forbid her to go camping.

The burning pain made for a sleepless night. Yet, she made no mention of it to Jerry. The next day, she was back on the playhouse project, moving a notch slower.

The kids were entertaining themselves with skateboards Daddy brought home from the dump. Their belly-surfing was slow-going on the rocky driveway; the kids were having a heyday. Michelle took one last glance at Caden as he scootered by, chuckled, and then headed over to the project site.

Today, she would start construction on the small screened-porch addition. The two-by-fours she was using also came from the dump. Matter of fact, their sauna, cabin, storage barn, and outhouse were almost completely built from salvaged materials. Michelle was no stranger at the dump. She was a frequent shopper. The roof on their cabin displayed seven different shingle colors. They were new shingles someone had saved but then decided to dispose of. There was not enough of any one color to do a roof. A fellow had seen Jerry shopping at the dump and asked if he was interested in his collection. The rest was history.

The screened porch and the new deck took a couple weeks to do, in between being a mother and a wife. Michelle's waistline was shrinking and her muscles were toning. Her shoulder, however, still burned inside and brought much silent discomfort.

The camping trip was one month away. Five women, including Michelle, were slated for the outing. Michelle asked three of the ladies to be in earnest prayer regarding a devotion they could each lead. She wanted the trip to be an encouraging time where the ladies could openly share of Christ's work in their lives. Michelle had an idea for her devotion, but the thought of giving it frightened her. She would have to pray more to make sure of God's leading.

CHAPTER SIX

D J

DJ was calling daily now, asking all sorts of questions about what kind of gear to have, what type of shoes would be best, and so on. The "California Kid" had no idea what BWCA camping was all about. Michelle was looking forward to going shopping with her. DJ was not the outdoorsy type.

DJ had been married and living in Minnesota for less than a year when she made a startling discovery. She stepped outside of her octagon-shaped home one autumn day, only to hear a strange noise. She could not put her finger on its source. She had never heard it before. It was not the sound of danger, but it was everywhere. She glanced around and saw nothing that was threatening. The only things moving were yellow aspen leaves falling to the earth. It clicked, for the first time in her life, that she was hearing the sound of deciduous leaves making their final journey, whirling to the ground.

Michelle knew the shopping trip would be comical. She would try to behave and not laugh in her friend's face. She would do that later with Jerry.

After the Sunday morning service, the Nylands invited the Paulsons over for the day. The anticipated shopping trip came to fruition. The ladies left their six kids in the care of their husbands.

Michelle and DJ were giddy as they chatted about the upcoming trip. The ladies walked through the Kmart camping section at a slow pace. This was more of a window-shopping trip. Michelle wanted to explain to DJ what she should look for in certain gear.

"Don't waste your money buying a plastic water bottle," Michelle said, stopping in front of the huge display. "Look for a poly-carbon type of bottle, like Nalgene. They're practically indestructible. They don't absorb odors. Your water will taste like water, not plastic. Thirty-two ounces is a good size. You'll want to be constantly drinking when you're out in the woods. Get a pretty colored one so you won't be able to tell the real color of your water. My water filter removes bacteria and viruses, not color."

As they neared the headlamps, Michelle spouted out some more pertinent information. "If you don't have a headlamp, I'd highly recommend one. It frees your hands to do dishes, read a book, go to the latrine, or even paddle a canoe. I don't bother with flashlights anymore. Cheap headlamps do the trick just as well as the more expensive ones."

"I am so glad you are explaining all this to me, Michelle. Brant would never take the time to educate me."

"No problem." Michelle was enjoying herself. She was talking and DJ was listening. Usually, it was the other way around.

"Make sure you have a good sleeping bag. It's common to see your breath in the morning. One with a fair amount of cushion is nice for the back too. Check the tags to see how 'cold' it's rated."

They walked over to the shoe department. DJ showed Michelle a very fashionable pair of shoes.

"They're nice for church but not practical for the Boundary Waters. I usually recommend bringing two pairs of shoes. One pair of breathable hiking boots that can get wet during the portages and one pair of comfortable sandals for camp and swimming. You'll for sure want to wear something on your feet when you swim. The rocky lake bottoms are unpredictable. They can be both sharp and slimy."

The ladies discussed raingear, fishing tackle, backpacks, sleeping pads, and a whole plethora of other things as well.

Time got away from the two friends. They needed to hurry back, make supper, and get out the door in time for the evening service. During the truck ride, DJ asked Michelle, "Is Jerry going on the guys' camping trip?"

"No. He doesn't know anything about it. When is it?"

"In two weeks. Jack is organizing it. They have one more opening available if Jerry wants it. Brant has been invited." DJ paused, "Actually, Jack told Brant, 'make sure you take these dates off, you're going camping with us.' They're going into the BWCA to Perent Lake. That's where they will camp and fish. The guys go there every year."

"So Brant is going then?"

"That's the weird thing; he hasn't really committed and said yea or nay. All I know is he's been invited."

"It would be great if Jerry could go. He needs guy-time, even if he doesn't think so. He gets in a social rut and doesn't make much effort to broaden his friendships. I would think he would get pretty bored of seeing just my face day after day. It sounds like we will have to exert some pressure on these men of ours to go fishing and relax a bit."

"Well, Social Director Paulson," DJ said in a business-like tone, "how hard could it be to convince the husbands to go play?"

"Humph. They're both broke, in lots of debt, behind in work, and need to pay bills. We could be in for a struggle."

A struggle was an understatement. The men were torn between work and relaxation. For two weeks they teetered back and forth. The two yo-yos finally bent to their wives' persistent pressure. The ladies had their husbands' best interest in mind. Both men were workaholics. Being self-employed, they had to be. They needed some R and R. Secretly, in the back of Michelle's mind, she knew that by Jerry going on this trip, he could not in good conscience make her feel guilty for going on hers.

CHAPTER SEVEN

A MAN'S MIND

Michelle took advantage of Jerry's absence on the guys'camping trip and stayed up till the wee hours of the morning. For almost nine years, the early-to-bed husband had stifled the night owl that lived in Michelle. The kids were put to bed early so Michelle could relish the evening hours behind a book. She chose to read *For Women Only* by Shaunti Feldhahn. This particular book had been saved for the special occasion of Jerry's absence. She needed to read it without him constantly interrupting, looking over her shoulder and asking what she was learning.

The book dealt with the inner lives of men, how they thought, and what made them tick. Michelle needed to deal with some issues in private. Now was the time. She had already put it off too long.

Her procrastination did not bury the uncomfortable subject; it only made her more bitter.

Had Jerry been home while she was reading the book, she would have felt like doing him bodily harm. He for sure would have received "The Look." She knew he would have found humor in the book and teasingly asked, "Have you learned anything new about me you didn't know?" Or he would have accusingly said, "You mean you didn't know that?" Michelle needed this time alone. Time to think, time to cool off. God was dealing with her. God finally had her attention.

A few days later, Michelle had cooled off enough to welcome her husband home with a big hug. She was glad to see him safe, refreshed, and with fish. She took the Ziploc of walleye from him, rinsed the fish, and stuck them in the refrigerator. She knew what she would make for supper. Michelle loved dining on walleye. She was resolved to play social director more often if it got her fresh fish.

The kids swarmed around Jerry, each one vying for his attention. When the kids had their fill of Daddy, the two adults settled down on the couch. Jerry had an eager audience. Michelle wanted details. He elaborated on the whitecaps that nearly capsized the canoe, the gunshots that almost killed them, and the big fish that got away.

"The start of the trip," began Jerry, "was rainy, cold, and terribly windy. Brant sat in the bow and received the brunt of the whitecaps. He was almost completely drenched. His head stayed dry because his baseball cap had protected it. With that being the only dry spot he could find, he stored his matches there."

"We canoed most of the lake, looking for an open campsite. Before we could find one, something zinged by my left ear. The noise didn't register immediately. Then, about two hundred yards behind us, we heard the sound of gunshots being sprayed wildly into the woods. It was either paddle or die. We put as much distance between the noise and us as we could. Fortunately, the whitecaps were pushing us to safety. I don't think we were purposely targeted; the shooters were probably some irresponsible kids."

Jerry did not dwell on the fact that he nearly faced death. He simply brushed it off and moved on to all his fish stories. The shooting incident bothered Michelle more than it did Jerry. Unknowingly, she tucked that story into her mental fear file.

"So, now that you've heard all about my trip, what did you do while I was gone?"

Avoiding eye contact, Michelle shifted uneasily in her seat. "I stayed up late each night reading a book."

"Oh, is that the book about men Joan lent you?"

"Yes."

"Did you learn anything new about me?"

Michelle flinched at the predictable question. "It all depends on how you answer some questions I have for you."

"What questions?"

That was her cue. Michelle nervously shooed the kids outdoors and cautiously proceeded to ask the questions that had been haunting her for years. Jerry's honesty confirmed her fear. Even though Michelle hated the answers she was getting, she appreciated the fact that her husband was being honest with her. Most men would have crumbled under this type of scrutiny. Michelle's mind was whirling. She would have to sort out her emotions later. For now, her growling stomach reminded her of the fish chilling in the refrigerator.

Two more weeks and maybe I'll be catching some fish of my own, she thought.

CHAPTER EIGHT

THE DEPARTURE

The next two weeks went by like both a turtle and a rabbit. At times, Michelle thought the trip would never get here. The next moment, she was worried she would not have enough time to get everything done. In preparation of the trip, she spent, more money than she had. She wanted everything to be perfect.

A new pump filter was purchased to ensure the safety of the drinking water. A camp stove griddle was bought to make pancakes. A Carlisle canoe paddle, a new headlamp, film, a canoe chair, and expensive water shoes were all put on the credit card. She did not buy everything in one shopping excursion. She spread it out over a week-and-a-half time period, hoping Jerry would not keep track of the total. He was not fooled. She decided he would first see her new water shoes after the trip was over. She could not return the shoes if they were already worn. Under normal circumstances, Michelle was not a big shopper. She preferred being a homebody rather than a mall-goer.

Michelle, however, was confident DJ would notice the new shoes and probably congratulate her for spending money on herself. If DJ had her way, she would take Michelle shopping and force her to buy a new wardrobe. Michelle's tomboyish outfits lacked charm. Secretly, DJ was embarrassed for her friend. To Michelle, having something new in her wardrobe meant raiding her husband's side of the closet. DJ once pressed the issue and asked, "Why don't you dress up more?"

"Money." Michelle simply answered. "We struggle just to buy groceries. New clothes are not an option." The topic made Michelle uncomfortable.

On the eve of the departure, Michelle worked herself into a migraine. Whether it was her nerves or something out of place in her neck, she couldn't tell. She had been very cautious that day after coming home from her chiropractic adjustment. Her mind, however, had not been cautious. She was struggling to rest and trust in the Lord, worrying that something—anything—would go wrong. She was running on fumes. Caden was sick and caused her to lose precious sleep. She was fearful he would not improve. Fearful that Jerry would not know how to care for him. Fearful Caden would end up in the hospital.

Her shoulder, bad weather, wild animals, stray bullets, forest fires, the whole kit and caboodle were resonating in her throbbing head. The thought of accidentally swallowing contaminated beaver water and contracting the flulike Giardia bug made Michelle sick to her stomach as well. Two Tylenol later, she still could not think straight.

"Jerry, I can't function. I need to go to bed. You're on your own with Caden tonight. I need at least one good night's sleep."

The radio announced Michelle's wake-up call at five o'clock. Her sleep had been adequate. Her clothes were set aside the night before and lay waiting for her. She put on her new Bugs Bunny Santa Claus socks. Santa Claus put a bad taste in Michelle's mouth, but she did not want to be wasteful and throw the socks away; a relative had given them to her. She decided to let them self-destruct on her camping trip.

Her army-green REI camping shorts had been given to her as well. They were extremely comfortable, made of a thin durable nylon, and would air dry quickly if washed. She sported her blue baseball cap and a pair of black canvas hiking boots. Michelle's shirt was not of her normal tomboyish attire. It was white with little flowers and a slight v-neck. It was not strikingly fancy, but it was prayerfully acquired.

Satisfied that the cabin was clean and in order for her husband, she double-checked the refrigerator and cupboards to make sure her family would not starve in her absence. When she prepared food for her trip, she made extra to leave behind to lessen the burden on her husband. With all the goodies in the refrigerator, Jerry would survive just fine. She shut the door with a contented smile.

Michelle brushed her teeth, packed the cold food items, kissed her sleeping husband, and headed out the door. She was meeting the ladies in town at six o'clock.

An early start was vital. The wind usually picked up speed as mornings progressed. They needed to cross a large lake on the first leg of their journey.

Parked outside of the Paulsons' rental unit in town, Michelle patiently waited. It was six thirty-five when the latecomers finally showed. DJ was visibly distressed at their tardiness but had been helpless to speed things along.

DJ spent the night at Jenna Cole's so she would not sleep in and be late. She wanted to be on time. Planning for this trip had put a spring in her step all summer. She looked forward to the day she could briefly paddle away from all the cares that consumed her world. Michelle listened patiently to the details of DJ's distraught explanation for their lateness.

A quick tour of the rental unit was given to the ladies. This was where the Paulsons held a mid-week Kids Bible Club. The reason for purchasing this building was due to the fact that the rent in their previous location had skyrocketed. It was more than they could afford. Upon seeing this duplex, they felt a peace about purchasing it. The building was well taken care of, and the rent from the second apartment would cover most of the mortgage. The same day they made an offer to purchase the property, another interested party also made an equal offer. The owner chose to accept the Paulsons' offer. She liked the fact that they were not in it for the money.

The apartment had a basement equipped with a laundry facility and shower. The main level consisted of a remodeled kitchen, dining room, and large living room. The upstairs held three bedrooms and a bathroom. The apartment was also used to put up guests, and one room had evolved into Jerry's office. Jerry used the property as his headquarters. Before work each day, he would hit the rental, have his quiet time, eat breakfast, and pack a lunch. He was also diligent to do any laundry Michelle might send with him.

Michelle locked the door behind everyone and headed for the truck. DJ rode with her. Jenna took her mother, Karen, and Annie Ojala in her van. The five women made a quick stop to pick up some Krispy Kremes and then headed to the International Wolf Center. The ranger's station was headquartered there.

They all went inside to procure the permit and watch the required video. A ranger briefly explained the regulations and then signed off, legalizing the paper Michelle would carry in her back pocket.

Todd, one of the rangers, was a snowplowing customer of Jerry's. He and Michelle chatted back and forth. Michelle ended the conversation by telling about Jerry's trip.

"A couple weeks ago, Jerry and DJ's husband, Brant, went into Perent Lake and were nearly shot to death." Michelle relayed the order of events to the surprised ranger.

"Please tell Jerry to come in and file an incident report," Todd begged. "We take these occurrences very seriously. We need to talk to him. Then we can investigate this. Please tell him to come in."

"I will tell Jerry what you said." With that the ladies bid their adieus and walked to the parking lot.

"I'm glad they had us watch that video," said Jenna. "Seeing the people bang on pots and pans to scare away the black bears really encouraged me. I don't know why, but I've been terribly scared of the creatures. I've never even seen one live in person. The video didn't make them look like the blood-thirsty beasts I've imagined."

The thirty-mile drive to Rock Lake took an hour of slow, cautious driving. The Echo Trail was notorious for its bumpy, windy road. Improvements were slow in coming to the ruggedly beautiful route. The two ladies, riding in Tucker, passed the time reminiscing about their trip to Rock Lake last Labor Day weekend. Both were eager to stand on its lovely shore once again.

Even though the lake had two resorts and a handful of cabins, people had to look hard to see any sign of them. The cabins were creatively tucked out of sight, with Carmen's cabin nearly invisible from the Lake.

Michelle pulled into the Rock Lake boat landing and parked her ruby-red truck. Jenna followed suit, parking her van in an open spot. So far, so good; no natural disasters, flat tires, or anything of that sort; they had made it this far. Michelle's nervousness, however, would not be dispelled until she was actually seated in her canoe, putting distance between her and the landing.

Michelle glanced out over the beloved lake. She beheld the large island, the rocky shoreline, and with a glance upward, the approaching storm clouds. With an unorganized haste, the ladies unpacked the canoes and the gear and waited patiently for Michelle's direction. The loud cracks of thunder did not faze the four greenhorns standing by the canoes. Their only worry was who would be going in which canoe. Michelle was troubled, and a worried look deepened on her face. She saw the ladies holding aluminum paddles, standing next to seventeen-foot-long aluminum lightning rods. The rain began to fall. At first a light drizzle, then a downpour. A truck towing a boat pulled into the parking lot. The driver got out and assessed the weather.

"You're not planning on heading out now, are you?" Michelle asked the stranger.

"No, I'll wait it out. The forecast I just heard said the front was momentarily passing through." He went back into the cab of his tuck and sat with his dog.

Michelle had heard that same forecast. "OK, ladies, leave everything out. Jenna, is it OK if we all wait in your van?"

"Sure, that would be fine."

Annie had just finished stuffing her unprotected sleeping bag into a plastic sack Jenna found for her. Everything else Michelle saw looked good and watertight.

"Shouldn't we load the gear back into the truck?" inquired DJ.

"No. Hopefully everything here is protected in plastic. It can stay out in the rain." Michelle again urged the ladies not to linger outside. "Every year someone gets struck by lightning up here. You had best get in the van." Lightning was not something she wanted to fool with.

When everyone was safely seated in the minivan, the windows quickly rebelled against the onslaught of wet, sweaty, warm bodies. The fogged-up windows blocked the women's melancholy view of the falling rain. As the downpour continued, DJ brought Michelle up to speed on the CD story they had started at the beginning of their trip. Dee Henderson's book, *The Negotiator*, had Michelle transfixed in no time. When the rain did stop, she was disappointed to leave the story.

"I'll need to borrow those CDs when you're done with them, DJ, but for now it looks like story time is over. It's slightly drizzling out, but I think we can handle that. The lightning seems to have passed." Michelle paused, and then added, "Before we leave the van, let's take some time to pray."

A prayer was said, and then the five women headed toward the lake. Everything in the canoes needed to be removed. The waterlogged crafts were overturned and freed of the rainwater.

"Michelle," DJ said quietly, "do you mind if I canoe with Jenna and her mom?"

"No, I don't mind. Thanks for asking, but you didn't need my permission," Michelle said trying to stifle a look of relief. Michelle had canoed with DJ once. Her slight frame had not lent much power to the forward motion of the canoe. DJ's fragile shoulders allowed only a few strokes here and there. On that trip, Michelle did not want to start DJ's vacation off with pain, so she graciously picked up the slack. The forty-five minute paddle to Carmen's cabin on a near-whitecap day had been a draining experience. DJ helped paddle only when they were in sight of the landing. Upon reaching the shore, Michelle could hardly stand. Her knees shook so bad from the tremendous amount of energy that was exerted. She had to lie down shortly after her arrival. Even running the Twin Cities Marathon had not robbed her of that much strength.

Since then, Michelle was aware of the fact that DJ was gaining endurance. Brant had been taking his wife canoeing on the lake near their home. Brant walked away from his camping trip with a healthy respect of whitecaps. He wanted to make sure his wife would hold up on her trip. He was worried. In confidence, he told Jerry, "I don't know what your wife is thinking by inviting DJ to go camping. Those whitecaps could kill her."

Jerry remembered how drained Michelle was after her canoe ride with DJ. He remained silent and chose not to tell Brant about the incident.

Michelle's smile deepened as she turned from DJ to face Annie, her new canoeing partner. She whispered a silent thank-you to God and added, "Can you put her in my tent, too?" Allusive Annie Ojala could not escape from Michelle now.

Jenna carefully seated herself in the bow of the Grumman canoe. A week before, it had been doubtful if Jenna could even go camping. She had dislocated her hip and put out her lower back. She could barely walk into the chiropractor's office. After a few adjustments, a little TLC from her husband, rest, and lots of prayers, she was back on her feet.

Michelle procured an extra canoe chair for Jenna to use; she wanted her to have more back support while paddling and sitting at camp. Jenna's back made Michelle nervous; she watched her like a hawk, making sure Jenna didn't overdo herself.

Karen was the duffer. She was sitting on the portage yoke when Michelle advised her to keep her weight lower in the canoe. "The canoe will be considerably more stable if you sit on the bottom rather than up high on the yoke. Oh, another thing, as the official duffer, you are exempt from having to paddle. Only paddle if you want to. Michelle gave the ladies some more helpful advice about steering, portaging, and what to expect on the first leg of the trip. She could not tell if her words registered with the ladies; they were acting like they were on a sugar-high, about to explode if they couldn't exert their pent-up energy.

Michelle straddled the canoe so DJ could take her place in the stern. When she was seated, Michelle shoved the three off in the Grumman. Next, she straddled her own canoe so Annie could crawl over the gear and onto the front seat. With Annie situated, Michelle pushed off and jumped in.

A drizzling mist and a slight wind welcomed the group to Rock Lake. Michelle and Annie, in the Alumacraft canoe, made good time paddling. They traveled a straight line in the direction of the first portage. The threesome in the other canoe, lagging behind, zigzagged everywhere. They could not boast a straight travel path or good time. Michelle and Annie slowed their pace. They were not in a race and had no need to hurry. Rock Lake was calm and not trying to kill them with whitecaps. That was Michelle's main concern in starting so early.

Michelle was breathing a little easier with each stroke she took. She started to relax and gather her thoughts. She noticed her partner's stiff silence. "What are you thinking about, Annie? You seem deep in thought."

"I was actually so deep in thought, I was drowning. I was just thinking about how nervous I am. I've never done anything this adventurous before without Mike. I'm scared, Michelle. What if I can't do this?"

"I know what you mean, I'm a bit nervous myself," Michelle said not knowing how many of her own fears to share with Annie. "Husbands are quite handy to have on camping trips. There's a sense of security with our strong protectors around. When I camp with Jerry, I let him do all the worrying, and I'm left without a care in the world. He does all the heavy grunt work and I'm left with the wimpy chores. It's kind of nice having some one spoil you like that. But I think you'll do just fine, Annie. I'm guessing you might even surprise yourself. Don't waste all your time worrying. The trip will be over before you know it. Enjoy the time without your two shadows."

Michelle was referring to Annie's children, eight-year-old Emma and four-year-old Eli. Annie had never left her kids home alone with her husband before. He had never spent a single night alone with them.

"Does Mike have big plans for the kids while you're gone?"

"That's just it; his mom volunteered to take the kids. He won't have to even see them if he doesn't want to."

"You're kidding!"

"No, I'm not."

The Grumman was still a bit behind, but they were catching up. Michelle and Annie sat silently idle. They listened to DJ trying to convince Jenna that she was supposed to help steer in the front. Jenna begged to differ. Michelle softly chuckled as she remembered her gentle admonition to the three ladies.

Before shoving off, Michelle had instructed the Grumman passengers to put the strongest woman in the back to steer. The forty-five-year-old Karen did not consider herself worthy of that position. That left Jenna and DJ to decide who would fill that seat. When DJ decided it should be her, Michelle bit her lip. She figured DJ would be humbled soon enough without her having to point out the obvious. Jenna, even with her bad back, had more arm strength than DJ.

Jenna's five-foot six-inch frame was not petite like DJ. She had a good solid build. Under normal circumstances, Michelle would not have worried about Jenna.

When the ladies were close enough, Michelle presented information on how to do the *J* stroke. "The person steering in the stern can turn the paddle in the shape of a *J* at the end of each stroke. Precious time is saved by this efficient steering method. The valuable stroke eliminates the time wasted in ruddering from side to side." With that bit of information, the two canoes parted, leaving DJ behind to practice.

The map sat in front of Michelle, balanced on her Duluth Pack. She squinted her eyes as she searched the shore for the portage entrance. The group had canoed in the gray mist for nearly an hour. It was time to leave Rock Lake behind.

CHAPTER NINE

THE PORTAGE

As they approached the little opening in the shoreline, Michelle's dread of the portage grew. She already knew that no one else could handle the canoes. She would be making two trips across the portage. Her anxiety was threatening to choke her. *Will my shoulder survive? What if Jenna's back goes out again? Could DJ hold up to this strain?* The 160-rod portage would be the toughest part of the trip. Portages were havens for big bugs; mosquitoes; wet undergrowth that slapped people in the face; narrow, rocky trails sometimes covered in mud, and slippery paths. The demanding portages brought out much complaining and shirking. They could also eat a lot of time if more than two trips across had to be made.

Michelle silently prayed for strength and paddled the canoe into the narrow muddy opening. They quickly emptied the canoe of its gear and moved the craft out of the way. The Grumman pulled in shortly after and the same process was followed. Jenna slowly evacuated the canoe; her tailbone was giving her grief.

"Ladies, I plan on making two trips across with the canoes. Without killing yourselves, see if you can do it in two trips as well. Make use of every free hand. The trail is going to be extremely slippery from the rain. Oh, and Jenna, please be careful. Don't overdue it."

After the brief exhortation, Michelle stood next to the Grumman, grabbed the portage yoke with both hands, and took a deep breath. In one swift motion she hoisted the canoe onto her shoulders. She carefully climbed the wet, rolling granite hill and slowly jogged with the canoe, wanting to make good time in case a third trip was necessary.

The mother/daughter team followed Michelle, loaded with as much gear as they could stand. Jenna wanted to see how much she could handle but had no intention of overdoing it.

DJ and Annie brought up the rear. Each wore her own personal backpack and carried fishing rods, paddles, and lifejackets. DJ stared up the slippery granite hill that introduced them to the 160-rod portage. Each step was carefully measured and executed. One wrong move could spell disaster. She had no intention of slipping and rolling down this hard hill. She could just imagine herself lying on her back like an upside down turtle at the bottom of the hill.

At the top, the rolling hill narrowed into a little granite path that beckoned her to follow. Ripe blueberry bushes lined the path as far as the eye could see. The tasty morsels were calling her name, but DJ purposed to only enjoy them with her eyes. She did not figure it would be too ladylike to bend over the bushes to feed her face; she had no desire to ruin her appetite before lunch. The hard granite trail turned into a crunchy brown carpet. Dead pine needles cushioned each step. The underbrush soon replaced the blueberries, and the wet leaves felt yucky when they touched DJ everywhere. "I dislike these little trees grabbing me with their wet fingers," she mumbled out loud to no one but herself. "*And,* I don't like giving these dreadful mosquitoes a free meal either." She set down her gear and rummaged through her pack to find her DEET-free bug spray. Annie caught up, and the two sprayed themselves. They reloaded and pushed forward.

The straps on DJ's pack dug into her shoulders. She could feel her blood vessels popping under the weight. "Yuck, I hate popped blood vessels," she proclaimed. The trail seemed to go on forever, and each step forward required more effort than the last.

DJ's overactive imagination was taking over. "I wonder if I'm lost. Maybe this is a never-ending deer trail taking me further into a desolate wilderness. Perhaps it's a trap with a hungry mountain lion waiting at the end of it. Hmm, I can see it now. The headlines will read: "Foolish Woman Lost in BWCA. Never Found. Husband and Three Children Left to Mourn." Maybe Michelle possesses a cruel sense of humor, purposely leading me out here to get lost. She's seeking revenge for all the years I've talked her head off. If I get out of this alive, I promise I will be a better listener."

The weight on her shoulders was making her delirious. She had to stop. DJ paused to remove her gear and was startled by Annie's presence next to her. Annie's twinkling eyes and soft smile told DJ her rambling had not been private. Annie rested next to her and picked up the babbling where DJ left it. Before their rest was over, they concocted the wildest story.

Moving on, DJ put her foolishness aside and purposed to make better mental use of her time. Michelle approached the two loaded pack animals and wished she had her camera with her. "You'll be able to see the lake soon, you're almost there. DJ? Do you have the time?"

She held her wrist in front of Michelle to see and said, "It's on military time."

"Why?"

"I like to do math" was her simple reply. "It keeps my brain young."

DJ had definitely missed her calling. She should have been an FBI agent. Her detail-oriented mind loved to sort out mysteries as well as create them. She could spend countless hours doing mind games, word finds, math story problems, and any type of mental puzzle she could get her hands on. She loved details. She could read a story and relay it back so accurately one would feel as though they read it for themselves. She could have been a valuable asset to the FBI. Michelle enjoyed DJ's detailed accounts. Sometimes she wondered, though, if a ninety-minute phone call could be condensed into a thirty-minute conversation instead.

Michelle saw it was nearly noon and then headed to retrieve the second canoe.

"Michelle!" DJ yelled after her, "How long is a rod?"

"A rod is the length of a canoe, about sixteen-and-a-half feet."

"Thank you."

"Sure thing." Michelle did not need to ask; she knew what would be going on in DJ's mind.

The second canoe was heavier than the first. The yoke pads were not properly spaced. They uncomfortably dug into Michelle's shoulders. She was not able to jog this time, but she did manage to finish the portage without having to stop for a break. Her brief rest came after the canoe was lowered onto the shore. She casually walked back down the portage to see how the ladies were fairing. She relieved Jenna and took the heavy pack to the canoe. The rest of the ladies arrived one by one and deposited their gear into the appropriate craft.

DJ announced to the group: "I have figured out that this portage is equivalent to 2,640 feet. Since we did the trip twice, walking that distance four times, we just walked a total of 10,560 feet." Michelle smiled at that tidbit of information she expected.

Everything was packed up into the right canoe. Amazingly, the ladies were still all in one piece. DJ survived and was not left to wander around lost in the woods. No one twisted an ankle, and everyone was in relatively good spirits.

DJ noticed the awful smell that permeated the air. "What is that terrible odor?"

"It's the muck. This is a swamp lake, only three-to-five feet deep. Maybe that's why they call it Pond Lake." Michelle went on, "We could eat lunch right here or paddle across the lake and eat at the campsite. While we're there, we can check out the site to see if we want to stay or press on."

The unanimous vote was to move on and eat lunch at the campsite. The ladies hoped the air there was fresher. Annie and Michelle pushed off leaving the Grumman behind. Determined not to ruin her new black leather shoes, Karen struggled to get into the canoe without mudding up her footwear. One shoe sank into the muck leaving the woman in a precarious position.

"Oh great! I just ruined one of my new shoes," she said with disgust.

"Mom! Didn't you listen to Michelle when she spoke to us back at the boat landing?"

"Why? What did I miss?"

"She told us to expect to get our feet wet and muddy on the portages. She also told us how she didn't like canoeing with people who were afraid to get their feet wet. She said that when someone pampers their feet they endanger the safety of the others in the canoe."

"Why would that put someone in danger?"

"Sometimes an emergency arises and it's necessary to hop out to free the canoe from the object it's stuck on or to steady it with your feet in the water so someone can safely enter or exit. Since babying your shoes, you've been tipping our canoe, and if you slip, you could cause us all to fall in. You'll be safer if you aren't worried about your shoes, Mom."

"Oh, all right!" Karen said as she stepped into the muck, immersing her remaining good shoe. "There! Are you happy now? Both of my shoes can get ruined together."

Not another word was said as they pushed off. Karen sat in a silent huff, not liking the fact that her daughter had rebuked her and was right. She examined her bad attitude and had to have a quiet talk with herself. When her attitude adjustment was complete, she admitted the wisdom in her daughter's words and purposed not to be so selfish. They paddled quickly trying to catch up to the Alumacraft.

Michelle noticed, as she traveled, that the shoreline of the weedy lake was almost completely vegetated by low-lying black spruce. There was one little hill with a small stand of pine trees. That's where the campsite was. Swimming in this lake would be out of the question. The very thought of it grossed Michelle out. The lake was depressing.

Michelle and Annie reached the granite landing first and explored the site while they waited for the others. The terrible swamp odor had not followed them; the air was definitely more palatable. The campsite would do in a pinch; it could be a good place to sleep if nothing else.

The others arrived and checked out the site as well. The ladies then converged on the landing. A blessing was said, and Michelle handed around the loaf of bread. The ladies took out the number of slices they wanted, and Michelle squeezed a tuna sandwich mixture out from a Ziploc bag. No utensils were dirtied. Pringle chips, cookies, water, fruit, and carrots rounded out the meal.

After the food pack was put back together, Michelle studied the map. "We have two choices. If you're tired, we can stay here. If you've got some oomph left, we can paddle a mile up the Portage River, do a small fifteen-rod portage, and see if the only campsite on Rice Lake is available. If it's taken, we are out of luck unless you want to go farther and do a 520-rod portage. Otherwise, we will have to backtrack and stay here." Michelle let the ladies discuss the options. It was unanimous. They would press on.

"According to the map, there is higher ground surrounding Rice Lake. That means there should be more pine trees. So in general, better scenery. The lake looks to be a couple feet deeper too; it shouldn't be as weedy. Oh, before I forget, are there any volunteers to take tonight's devotion?" Silence.

"I guess I'll do mine tonight, but please be prepared to do yours the following day."

They pushed off and headed toward Portage River. Michelle was proud of the ladies. They had done a good job of packing light; they left the curling iron, makeup, and kitchen sink at home. The ladies were also successful in completing the portage in two trips. The big bonus in Michelle's mind was that no one had mutinied. The rest of today's journey should be a breeze.

Grassy reeds that slowed the canoes down to a crawl overran the mouth of the river. "I sure hope the whole river isn't like this, or else that 160-rod portage might seem like a cake walk." Michelle's fear was put to rest as the narrow river opened to a clear winding path for the travelers. A nice steady pace ensued. The atmosphere was lighthearted as Annie and Michelle visited and joked back and forth. Michelle kept feeling her forehead though, wondering if she was coming down with Caden's fever. She kept getting warmer. She noticed Annie removing her jacket and asked, "Are you warm?"

"Yes, it's getting uncomfortable out."

Relief flooded over Michelle; it wasn't just her. The clouds hid the sun, giving the impression that it should not be so hot. "Hold up a bit, Annie. Let's wait and get a picture of the other canoe."

"OK."

DJ had been humbled. Jenna, proving to be the strongest paddler, was sitting in the stern, while DJ duffed, and Karen sat in the bow. At the same instant, both Karen and Jenna pointed to a pretty tree and simultaneously said, "Look at that! Isn't that so beautiful?" DJ broke out laughing at the oneness of this mother/daughter team; they were so alike, it was scary. The three paddled around the bend toward the waiting camera. Photogenically they smiled, got their picture taken, and moved on.

Michelle was on a water bandwagon. "Make sure you gals drink enough; I have a feeling we're in for a scorcher. I'm thanking God for these clouds right now. Without them, it could be downright dangerous." If the clouds disappeared, Michelle would be driving the water bandwagon hard. None of the ladies were big water drinkers, so Michelle's reminders were helpful.

The heat did not bother Jenna; she was quite tolerant of hot temperatures. As she sipped on her water jug, she remembered her OCB "bee" days and the dangerously hot conditions she worked in. When she had lived in the Twin Cities, she found employment at the local Old Country Buffet. Her baker's position paled in comparison to that of being the company's bee mascot. She begged and pleaded with her boss, falling short of groveling on her knees, to be put in the mascot position. Under Jenna's steady pressure, her employer crumbled and gave her the coveted job. She did not need the extra hours the job required to work birthday parties, special occasions, and parades; Jenna was not in it for the money. It was not a glamorous job to dress up in a bee suit with a head as big around as her shoulders and a hula-hoop waist that could fit four of her inside. The position gave her a freedom that regular life lacked. Her wild side loved being paid to be goofy. Her bee antics brought joy to many youngsters as she waddled around hamming it up, and she really provoked the giggles when she would wiggle the big black behind. On scorching hot parade days, Jenna would wrap up in ice cubes before entering her suit. The ice helped to keep her cool in the big heat trap. It was a hot, sweaty job, but she tolerated the heat well.

DJ's chatter brought Jenna's mind out of her OCB bee days as the conversation turned to the approaching portage. The little river had proved to be quite pleasant, and the ladies were sad to see the relaxing stream end. A small, fifteen-rod rapid needed to be portaged around. With such a short distance, three trips across could be permitted. There was no need to push it when their destination was so close.

Halfway through the portage, a tree angled down over the path. With the canoe on her shoulders, Michelle had to crawl on her knees to get under. Three trips later, the ladies were once again pushing off. The shallow rocks hung the canoes up, making it difficult to depart. Michelle had to get into the water to help shove off the canoes, while the ladies, sitting in the canoes, helped push with their paddles. It was a team effort to dislodge the canoes. When they were freed from the rocks, they headed around the bend with great anticipation. Rice Lake appeared before their eyes.

CHAPTER TEN

RICE LAKE

The lake was beautiful to behold. It was a jewel after experiencing Pond Lake. One glance toward the empty campsite told them it was all theirs. Michelle's smile sprouted, and a prayer of thanksgiving was whispered. She was grateful they would not need to backtrack. Coming this far had been a gamble, but it was worth it.

The Grumman lagged behind Annie and Michelle. Karen was not feeling well. She should have been home recovering from two root canals; instead, she talked her dentist into putting off the procedure until after her trip. She had looked forward to this trip and did not want to miss it. Her dentist sent her off with extra penicillin and a package of powerful painkillers. "You can never have enough penicillin in the BWCA," he said. He also warned Karen not to overdo it with the painkillers. "You might see pink elephants, hallucinate, or even act like a wild animal if you take one. Only use these babies if you're dying." The way Karen was feeling, she should have consumed one of the deathbed pills, but she feared the consequences. She could just see herself out of control and acting like a maniac, embarrassing her poor daughter in front of her friends. She had embarrassed her daughter enough in the past; she could not bear the thought of doing it again. Karen suffered in silence.

The Alumacraft clipped along; they were eager to explore their new home. Upon reaching the shoreline, it was hard to decipher exactly where the landing was. Annie steadied the canoe so Michelle could jump out, explore, and find the landing. Within a minute, she was signaling Annie to drift further down to the right. The canoe and its contents were brought ashore to make room for the approaching Grumman.

When Karen's wet feet touched the shore, she clasped a Ziploc bag containing a roll of toilet paper in her hand and made a mad dash to find the latrine. She ran along what she hoped was the correct trail and was startled to see a grouse running alongside of her. *At least I'm seeing some wildlife*, she thought. What she really wanted to see was the latrine, and after that, a moose.

Annie and Michelle felt like a giddy Lewis and Clark as they explored the spectacular site. The campfire grate was nicely located up on a granite ledge among a stand of middle-aged white pines.

The view of the lake was as close to breathtaking as they could have hoped for. In front of the grate, the granite ledge dropped straight down seven feet, making a beautiful spot for a tent. Fifteen-feet behind the campfire grate was another level spot for a second tent. The first spot was by far the best. It was close to the lake with a great view. The fiberglass throne, more properly called the latrine, was quickly located and used. A roll of toilet paper in a Ziploc bag was left next to it.

Ripe blueberries and raspberries were so thick that in spots the ladies had to trample them to get where they needed to go. It was a blueberry-picking dream for Jenna. She had a love for blueberries and was known to drive hours to find a good picking spot. She would stay in a patch till she could pick no more or ran out of pails to fill. The nibbling started. Michelle wondered if the ladies would save some room for supper.

There were a lot of chores that needed to be done before nightfall. Michelle wanted to keep things moving. "Jenna, where would you like to set up your tent?" Michelle already knew where she wanted to set up hers but instead would let Jenna pick first. Jenna's comfort was more important.

"I'll take the spot down below the campfire, if that's OK."

"It's fine with me," Michelle said as she handed Jenna the extra air mattress she brought for her. "I hope this Thermarest will be helpful for your back. It's quite comfortable."

"Thank you, Michelle."

"Sure," she said as she turned to set up her tent. She wasn't sure how to best position the tent to avoid the annoying rocks that plagued her spot. She sighed and just threw the tent on and set it up. She would have to adjust her sleeping pad inside to avoid the bigger rocks. Michelle was not sure who her tent mate would be. She would let the chips fall where they may. Michelle did not have to wait long. Annie approached.

"May I bunk in with you, Michelle?"

"Of course you can, but I'm warning you, my husband says I snore." Annie laughed and set up her sleeping bag and Michelle whispered another silent thank-you to God. Jenna's tent was larger than Michelle's and would comfortably fit the other three women. With Annie's quiet nature, Michelle was confident she would get a good night's sleep, and oh, did she need it tonight. She was already exhausted.

Other chores needed to be done now that the tents were established. Jenna and Karen paired up to gather firewood. DJ was instructed to find a tree to hang the food pack from and get the rope in place. Michelle and Annie would take the canoe out to pump drinking water. Michelle watched Jenna and Karen pick up the hatchet and head off into the woods; she could tell they enjoyed each other's company. They talked and joked together as if they were best friends. An outsider would never guess the pair to be related and certainly not to be a mother/daughter team.

DJ was a sight to behold. She grabbed the rock that Michelle had tied on to the end of the rope and repeatedly threw it overhand, trying to lob it over a tree limb. She did not give up. It wasn't until she switched to an underhand toss half an hour later that she accomplished her mission with pride. Michelle was glad DJ had been so eager. She was worried that she might have injured her one good shoulder had she tried.

The sky was still overcast with the temperature somewhere in the nineties. The canoe sat a good distance from shore with Annie and Michelle in it pumping water. Annie handed Michelle multicolored containers one after another. *The ladies will be glad they can't tell the true color of their drinking water,* thought Michelle. The pumped water was pure and safe but unappetizing to look at. It was a dirty brown color. Michelle, knowing the true color, would have to be diligent to force herself to drink. It would not take long before the filter would be clogged. The pumping continued amidst their conversation.

"Annie, I want to tell you something, but I don't want you to take it the wrong way. Last month, when I saw Mike at church with you, my jaw nearly hit the floor. I couldn't believe it was him. He looks so different. He's very handsome with that hair cut."

"I know. My attraction for him has really grown since he cut his hair."

"What caused him to cut it? It must have been two feet long."

"I don't know how long it was, but I never liked it. I had thrown lots of hints at him that maybe he should cut it and see what short hair looks like. He never paid attention to my hints, so I gave up. Then one day I looked out my window and saw a stranger walking around outside. I thought it was one of Mike's friends. You can imagine how big my eyes got when I realized it was Mike. I ran outside and asked him to take his cap off, thinking the hair would fall down from under it, but it was gone. Trying not to show my true emotions, I asked him why he cut it. He said he had gotten a coupon in the mail and thought he'd use it. That was good enough for me."

"Is Mike going elk hunting again this year?"

"Yes, but this time he says he's only going for three weeks."

"I was pretty worried about you last time he left. You looked so lonely."

"He was gone for two months, Michelle. I've never been lonelier in my whole life. The cell phone only worked when he climbed to the top of the highest hill. From the lack of his calls I didn't know if he was dead or alive or even when he would come back. I ran out of money and had to borrow from my dad. I should have been furious to finally see him, but I was just so thankful to know he wasn't dead. He didn't even have an elk to show for all that time away. The hardest part was not knowing what to tell the kids when they asked when Dad would be coming home. It was a very dark time in my life."

"What drew you to Mike?"

"We had always been friends, but I never really fell in love with him. Even when we got married I wasn't in love with him."

"Really? Why did you marry him then?"

"To be honest, I felt trapped. We already had Emma out of wedlock. I couldn't live with my parents, not with a kid. My dad made that clear. I had no one else to help me get on my feet. I had nowhere else to turn. When Mike proposed, I felt I had to accept. I've had to learn to love him. Everything I feel for him now has come because I have chosen to focus on his good characteristics. The more I focus on those, the more my love for him grows. And to be honest, I'm crazy about him now. I can't imagine life without him. My love for him has been a decision, not a feeling."

"I suppose," Michelle spoke thoughtfully, "that's how God loves us. He looks at the good things about us, mainly His Son dwelling in us, and doesn't let the bad traits overwhelm Him. We definitely don't deserve God's love."

"No, we don't. I'm glad He loves us anyway.
Silence.

Michelle was deep in thought. She wanted to share something with Annie but did not know how to. Michelle was thinking about her husband. She had recently allowed herself to fall all the way in love with him.

Since their marriage in 1996, almost nine years ago, Michelle had held back part of her heart. She really did love Jerry. It was more than just a decision. It was also a feeling. Michelle, however, had been quite on her own before knowing Jerry. Buying her first house at age eighteen, adding eight additional acres of forestland at age twenty-one, and owning her own sign-carving business had given her a great sense of independence.

Coming to accept Christ at age nineteen had shaken her world. She struggled to give her independence to Christ and to learn to trust and depend on Him. The independence issue was something Michelle wrestled with daily. She liked being her own boss.

This inward struggle caused the Paulsons' first year of marriage to be a rough, rocky one. Michelle had proceeded to be the boss of her sign-carving business, not wanting interference from her husband, while Jerry worked hard to establish his own handyman business. He had requested his wife's help; her refusal wore Jerry out with long, rough days of working alone.

After a miserable, tense year of marriage, Michelle yielded and set aside her sign business, which had become a thorn in her flesh. Her decision turned the tide of their marriage. They worked hard together and made a great team. The marriage grew better with each passing year, but Michelle still had hidden independence. It held her heart back from totally serving Jerry out of love; instead, she worked with him, serving him out of duty.

He once asked her, "How come you don't smile as much anymore?"

Do I have to smile when I do my duty? she thought but voiced it not. The once carefree and bubbly woman had turned into a serious, stoic-faced wife and mother who secretly struggled to hold on to a small thread of independence. Her miserable attachment to independence robbed her of joy. Only recently had she come to the place of honesty. The truth had set her free.

Sitting silently in the canoe, her carefree spirit soared with her new freedom in Christ. Verses from John chapter eight were echoing in her mind. "And ye shall know the truth, and the truth shall make you free…If the Son therefore shall make you free, ye shall be free indeed."

Michelle went on to think about the devotion she would give tonight. It would not be easy to share what she had on her mind, but God was giving her the green light. She would simply have to claim Philippians 4:13 to get her through.

Annie was speaking, but it did not register with Michelle. "I'm sorry, what did you say?"

"I said we've drifted across the whole lake. The ladies might be thirsty. We should get the water jugs back to them."

"You're right; we have been gone a long time." Michelle enjoyed visiting with Annie and did not want it to end. Reluctantly, she began paddling.

When they arrived back at camp, a healthy stack of wood sat next to the fire grate. If the weather did not change, a fire would be out of the question tonight. Jenna and DJ were in the tent going over many scriptures with Karen. Michelle and Annie heard the important conversation inside and did not want to disturb the tide of its flow. They quietly left the area with fishing rods in hand.

Walking over blueberries, they headed to a granite bluff, sat down, and prepared the rods. While their bobbers floated motionlessly on the water, the ladies nibbled on the neighboring berries. Michelle turned just in time to see her bobber dance. Excitedly, she reeled in her line, only to be disappointed at the sight of a tiny little perch. She carefully freed the little Perca flavescens and watched it swim away. Another night crawler was put on the empty hook and a nice cast was made. Michelle settled into her "Sit Backer" chair, and turned her attention to Annie. "So what's the most outdoorsy adventure you've ever tackled?"

"This."

"Besides this?"

"Well, the extent of my camping has been limited to plush campers. So I guess that doesn't qualify as rugged. The only thing really challenging that comes to my mind is a recent hiking trip Mike took the family on." The thought of the trip made Annie's feet ache all over.

"Mike paid a lot of money to buy me a good pair of Danner hiking boots. I had worn them before to break them in and I ended up with painful blisters on both feet. The blisters hadn't quite healed when

Mike decided to take the family trip. We drove up the North Shore of Lake Superior and got a hotel room. Mike had his heart set on hiking to the highest point in Minnesota. It was a seven-mile round trip. The hike would prepare him for elk hunting in the mountains. Nothing was going to stop him from doing the entire hike.

"He gave me the option of staying at the hotel if I didn't think I could handle the hike. I didn't want to stay at the hotel and be bored, so I went. Mike carried Eli on his shoulders. Emma and I hiked behind. I didn't think to put BAND-AIDs on my old blisters before leaving. About halfway up the little mountain, I had to stop. My feet were killing me. I couldn't go on. I took off my boots. My feet were a bloody mess. I didn't know what to do. Mike was in a hurry to press on, so he said I could go back down and wait in the car or just wait right there until he came back. I wasn't going to get any sympathy from him, but I had no intention of giving up. I didn't go that far just to quit."

There was a stubborn sparkle in her eyes. Michelle liked that and smiled. "So what did you do?"

"I tied my boot laces together and slung them over my shoulder. I hiked to the top of that hill in my socks. Mike gave me the idea to put my boot insoles inside my socks, and that helped with some cushion. Mike was sorry he had wasted all that money on my expensive boots. I guess I was quite a sight, carrying two-hundred dollar boots instead of wearing them."

In disbelief, Michelle erupted into uncontrollable laughter. Her sides hurt. Moments later, she calmed down. "So you hiked halfway up and all the way down in your socks?"

"Yep."

More laughter.

"Was it worth it?"

"I was kicking myself that I didn't bring my camera. The view at the top was spectacular. I was glad I didn't give up. I would do it again, just not any time soon. I want to make sure my feet are 100 percent before I do anything like that again."

"Did Eli walk at all?"

"No, Mike carried him the whole way. When we were done, that silly boy complained that his feet hurt. Go figure."

"How did Emma do?"

"She was a real trooper. We hardly knew she was there. She didn't complain at all."

"Wow! That's impressive."

"For the most part I didn't complain either. I didn't want Mike to regret taking me. He rarely includes the family on his hunting and hiking trips. I wish he would take us more."

Mike was a good hunter, an outstanding hunter. He spent every spare moment in the woods with a rifle or bow or on a lake with a fishing rod. He hunted anything that was in season. His flexibility and drive to hunt caused him to be away from his family more than Annie desired. Not only was Mike's family time sacrificed, so was church and fellowship with other believers. Annie was often left being both mom and dad, the spiritual leader, comforter, teacher, and disciplinarian.

Annie had been a full-time mom but grew tired of not having enough money to buy necessities for the family. Every time she needed money, it was the same old story. Her name was not included on the checkbook, she was not allowed to use credit cards, and was totally dependent on Mike's fluctuating income. Annie felt guilty begging Mike for money. She had no means of supplying for her needs. Annie went back to school to get her nursing degree. In one more year, she hoped her begging would cease.

Annie had guts for going back to school at her age. Even though she was not a traditional student, her youthful appearance could easily pass her off as a teenager. Along with stubborn determination, her character was softened with sweetness. However, her sweetness tended to make her a bit naïve. For the first several years of marriage, Annie had no idea they annually received a large income tax return. When Annie's sister asked her how much their income tax return was, Annie admitted she knew nothing about the matter, but she later pressed Mike on the subject. She was quickly educated and quite surprised to learn about the money.

Michelle knew how sweetly naïve Annie was. With a strength that wasn't her own, she resisted the temptation to try to fool Annie into thinking there were dangerous "water bunnies" inhabiting these lakes. Her cruel water bunny joke had claimed many fools. Even the skeptical could be seen looking more closely at the water as they paddled along with Michelle. As a teenager on a church-led Boundary Waters trip, Michelle had once fallen victim to the scary thought of little bunnies with big teeth that swam under water. The joke had been on her. Now she enjoyed turning the table. It took an incredible amount of will power to leave unspoken the fabled creature. Michelle smiled and savored the thought of what could have been. Michelle wanted Annie's trust more than a good laugh.

The bobber jigged its little dance again. "Looks like another little perch," Michelle said dryly. DJ approached from behind and joined the two. Seeing a little sign of life in the water, she eagerly plopped her line in the lake, after Michelle put a worm on her hook. "Hope you took notes, DJ. I am only doing this for you once."

"I just don't have the heart to pierce the little creatures for myself, but if I have to I'll adjust."

This time DJ's bobber came to life. Michelle had to extract the hook from the perch's tiny mouth. "Hope you're still taking notes; the next one is yours to remove."

Michelle wanted fresh fish. She did not, however, have the patience to work for it. With no sign of anything edible, she gave up the hopes of a fish supper and adjusted her mind for hotdogs. It was time to start supper. The ladies picked up their gear and walked back to camp. Jenna and Karen were bending over a bush, eating berries just off the trail.

Michelle did not think it was healthy to eat so many berries in one day but said only, "Save some room for supper." The ladies were also guilty of indulging in sweets that day.

Michelle proceeded to the kitchen. Her kitchen area consisted of three large logs for seating, shaped in the letter C. The campfire grate was placed on the open end of the C, facing the lake. Michelle stood in her kitchen and looked out over the beautiful scenery. A couple of young white pines bordered the view. Annie entered the kitchen looking for directions, wanting to be helpful. Michelle set out the cookware and eating utensils, balancing them on top of one log. "You could find the hotdogs for me if you want. They're in that bucket over there under the tree. Please grab the potato salad too."

"Sure thing." Annie found the items and set them next to Michelle.

Priming the camp stove, the chef looked up at Annie. "The ketchup and mustard should be in that green pack. Could you grab those too?"

Annie did the task quickly. "Oh, and I need this pan filled with lake water for washing our hands." Annie disappeared without a sound. She reappeared with the pan of water.

"Thank you."

"Anything else?"

"No. The rest is pretty easy. I just need to watch the hotdogs cook."

Annie found a seat nearby in case she was needed. DJ was on her way to the tent when she noticed her bait sitting out in the sun. She opened up the Styrofoam container of worms, poked around in the dirt, and looked longingly at the wriggling crawlers. She was imagining the tasty fish meal they might supply. "Michelle, should I give the worms some water?"

"I think they are OK, but you might want to move your babies into the shade."

"All right. I have never bought worms before, so I'm not sure how to take care of them." DJ left for her tent after moving the worms.

Having consumed enough berries, Jenna sauntered into camp and spied the worm container. She too poked her finger in the dirt and declared, "It's dry. I think they need water."

Michelle bit her lip when she saw all the water Jenna poured into the container. Michelle was getting tired of hearing her own voice. She thought she was sounding too bossy. Saying nothing, she backed off and watched. The worms, desperate to flee their flooded home, were crawling out of the container. Jenna saw the escapees, put them back in, and repositioned the lid. A rock was securely placed on top for extra assurance.

Michelle was imagining the little guys taking their last dying breath. Their silent plea for help went unheeded. The cruel hard rock had sealed their fate. *Good thing Jenna didn't remember the second worm container down by the canoes,* she thought, holding back a secret smile. Michelle's growling stomach reminded her to check on supper. The hotdogs were done and plenteous; the worms were forgotten.

Michelle was disappointed when the meal was over and the pan was still full of hotdogs. Between the heat and all the snacking, the ladies hardly touched the meal. "I guess we're going to find out if seagulls like hotdogs," Michelle said, staring into the pan. Annie put the hotdogs in the canoe; they would later be transported to a neighboring island and left for the birds.

CHAPTER ELEVEN

SLIME

With the kitchen tidied up, Michelle put her swimsuit on and went down to the lake to clean up. The slimy rocks and brown water did not appeal to her. She hated touching slime with her feet and hands. She wanted to jump in and soak for a while, before scrubbing up. She thought better of it. Using an aluminum cooking pot, she repeatedly scooped up water and dumped it over her body. She soaped up and walked into the woods to rinse off. The rinsing took several trips. It was a BWCA rule that any soapy water be deposited 150 feet away from the lake.

A good swim would have felt nice, but she was not brave enough to launch off from this shore. It was gross. An idea lighted her eyes. She walked back to camp and convinced the other four women to suit up and follow. The five ladies fit into the canoe that held the hotdogs. They shoved off and headed for the little seagull island. Carefully, they parallel parked along the huge rolling boulder that was the island. As Michelle drug the bow onto the shore, the seagulls flew away, not liking the intrusion. The hotdogs were unceremoniously put down next to a couple old fish skeletons.

"We'll have to come back tomorrow and see if the birds liked their treat," Michelle said as she gave the island a quick three-second exploratory glance. She then moved to examine the shoreline more closely. It was thick here with slime as well, but she did find a spot where she could hopefully push off and not touch bottom. Michelle felt a little braver with the ladies watching. If she did not do this, she knew the others wouldn't either.

Imagining herself to be a water spider gliding on the surface, she pushed off from shore. Even with her water shoes on, she was careful not to let her feet drop too low in the water. She hated the thought of hitting something slimy. Floating on her back in the lukewarm brown water was not as refreshing as she had hoped. "Annie, could you please push the canoe out to me. Make sure its empty first. I want to see if I can get in it from the water."

"Sure. Do you want a paddle in it?"

"That'd be great, thanks."

Michelle did not want to try getting out of the lake on the icky shore. The canoe was a desperate attempt to avoid the slime. It took a bit of effort, but she managed to maneuver her way into the canoe without swamping it. She sat safely in the canoe feeling as though she had victoriously won a major battle over the slime monster. Michelle needed a good laugh. She urged the others to get wet.

The ladies were hesitant, not knowing if Michelle was serious or not. The ninety-degree heat convinced them it was a good idea. They were not as fortunate as Michelle. Each lady got slimed trying to get in, touching many thickly-coated rocks on the bottom.

DJ swam further out hoping the lake would deepen. She kept hitting hidden rocks just below the surface. "Eww. Yuck. Ouch. I hit another one." She was not having fun.

Michelle stifled a laugh and used her paddle to check the depth. At three and a half feet she hit bottom. Pushing the paddle harder, she gauged the slime to be another foot thick. Everywhere Michelle paddled and checked it was the same story. "The map did show that the lake was shallow." The ladies swam with their lifejackets on and were able to float effortlessly. They had no intention of going back the way they came.

"You could swim back to camp, it's not all that far," suggested the lone canoeist.

Annie did not like the suggestion. "Michelle, can you help me get in the canoe?"

"Sure, just don't swamp me. I'll try to balance out your weight." The others came to help. They spread themselves out around the canoe and held on.

Annie had a hard time but eventually made it into the floating haven of rest. As Jenna, Karen, and DJ swam for shore, they found humor in their predicament. Their lifejackets kept them from any serious harm. Their spirits were in adventure mode.

"My husband will not believe me when I tell him I went swimming." DJ was not a swimmer. Her first time in a canoe with Michelle had revealed her deep fear of water. A good lifejacket had been on her shopping list, and with it on, she felt secure in its embrace. "Too bad we don't have our cameras with us, then I could show Brant the proof. Oh well. My boys will just love this part of the story." DJ was already formulating in her mind how she would retell her great swimming adventure. She knew the slimy rocks would gross the kids out. She could already see their faces full of expression.

The canoe stayed close to the swimmers. The ladies took their time, dreading the inevitable. Getting out of the lake was tricky. There were no slime-free avenues of escape. Michelle felt guilty as she sat in the canoe and watched the hilarious exodus. When the ladies were safely on shore, Michelle let her suppressed laughter loose. It had been fun for her to see grown women squeal, squirm, and facially express their dread of the slime they were forced to touch. Michelle would have acted the same way had she been amongst them, and she knew it.

When they had all finished drying off and changing clothes, Michelle urged them to drink water. It was still extremely hot out, and the group had just exerted a tremendous amount of energy. While Michelle, DJ, and Annie were consuming their brown lake water, the mother/daughter team was secretly relishing the last remaining sips of town water. Karen's hydration pack still held some of the precious clear liquid from home. It was quickly consumed and replaced with the filtered brown lake water. Knowing they needed to drink more, they forced down the brown. It really did not taste bad; it just looked awful. Knowing the color, they grimaced with each forced swallow.

There was one more group chore that had to be done before Michelle could go out fishing at dusk. "If you gals want to eat anything else tonight, please do it now. In a few minutes we will hang the food pack. I will need all your personal snacks to be put in the pack for the night as well." A last minute feeding frenzy broke out. Lots of sweets were consumed. Michelle stayed away from the snacks and watched the others eat. She consumed enough at supper and was not hungry; besides, she knew how sugar messed her up on camping trips.

Personal snack-packages appeared from every direction and were piled into the food pack. The pack was tied to the rope along with the bread bucket, the cooler pail, and the garbage bag. It took the cumulative strength of all five campers to hoist the bundle. Two ladies handled the rope and pulled, while the rest lifted and pushed the pack into the air. Canoe paddles were used to push the load the rest of the way. The pack dangled ten feet up in the air.

The tree was the best they could find, but if a bear was truly hungry, Michelle feared the pack would be easy prey. She hoped that if a bear came into camp, it would prefer the less challenging blueberries that covered the ground below.

There was no doubt in Michelle's mind a bear could easily climb the tree and pull down the pack. She would have liked a sturdier branch that could handle the weight further out, but it was not so. She would have to trust the Lord to guard their precious food. *Good thing the forest is covered with edible berries should something happen,* she thought.

With the day's final chore accomplished, Michelle grabbed her pole and met DJ down by the lake. Michelle picked up the container of night crawlers that had not fallen victim to "Jenna the Worm Slayer." They pushed off in the canoe and drifted away from shore. Hooks were fitted with bait and plopped into the water.

DJ was getting used to baiting the worms and was enjoying the stillness of the early evening. The temperature was dropping; it felt wonderful. She was hoping to catch a big one. She would enjoy telling her boys about the experience, should it happen. The only fish she ever caught was the tiny perch that had made her bobber dance earlier in the day.

Her thoughts drifted to her silent fishing partner. It was bizarre that Michelle and she were friends. They were both so opposite. She was into clothes, fashion, makeup, shopping, being indoors, computers, and reading. Michelle hardly knew how to turn a computer on, was tomboyish, and disliked being inside; her only drive was to wear the aroma of the outdoors and to make sawdust. Under normal circumstances, there would have been nothing to bind their lives together. When DJ first met Michelle, she wasn't sure she even liked her. The two ladies simply endured each other for the sake of their husbands, who already were good friends. Their bond in Christ was all that had cemented their earlier friendship. Now, the two friends could freely bounce ideas off of each other and found that their differences actually enhanced the friendship. They learned from each other.

A couple little perch teased the women and made off with the worms. Michelle wasn't too disappointed in the lack of big fish giving her attention. She did not care to clean fish in the dark and to have to lower the cooler pail to put the fillets in. The sky was cloudless and the sun had totally disappeared from view. As hot as the day had been, it was now going to the opposite extreme. It was getting chilly out. If the temperature kept dropping, they would soon be able to see their breath.

The lack of any breeze empowered the mosquitoes, making the two fisherwomen easy targets. The ladies were forced to head back to camp. Michelle steered the canoe in the direction of the little campfire Jenna and Karen had started. Back at camp, Michelle and DJ found the others huddled around Jenna's burning citronella sticks. The sticks were useless against the onslaught of bloodthirsty mosquitoes. Visions of sitting around the campfire, singing, visiting, and enjoying the stars were shattered and carried away by the thick cloud of bugs.

"Is that a freeway I hear?" Karen asked puzzled. "I heard the noise start as soon as it got dark. It's like a low, rumbling road noise. Don't you hear it?"

"There are no freeways or roads anywhere near here," Michelle assured Karen.

"Mom, I hate to tell you this, but I'm pretty sure your freeway sound is the swarm of mosquitoes that descended on us at dusk."

"No way!" declared Karen in disbelief.

"I don't know how much longer I can force myself to stay outside," Michelle commented. She did not want to spray smelly bug dope on before retiring for the night. "Jenna, will your tent be available for devotions tonight?"

"It's all yours."

"Do you all plan on staying out much longer?"

"No, I think we're all tuckered out." Jenna answered Michelle for everyone.

"I would like to have devotions soon, if that's OK. I'm fading fast. How about we meet in ten minutes?" There were no objections. The ladies had enough time to brush their teeth and hit the latrine. Michelle's nerves were tensing up as she went to find her Bible and notes. She was shaking and had to calm down.

"Dear Lord," the silent prayer began. "You've shown me to share this, now please give me the calm strength to do so. I ask this in Jesus' name, Amen."

The prayer was not long, but it accomplished its mission. The quiet peace of God that passes all understanding put her nerves to rest. She reminded herself, *I'm only sharing how God has been real to me lately*. Even at that, she would be opening herself up, exposing an area of fault. To admit being wrong was hard for her. There was no turning back now. She was resolved to move forward in her walk with Christ.

CHAPTER TWELVE

THE DEVOTION

Someone from inside zipped open the tent so Michelle could enter. It quickly zipped shut behind her; everyone was there. A handful of mosquitoes also entered and were efficiently hunted down. The atmosphere was quiet and serious as they waited for Michelle to begin.

"I'd like to start with a word of prayer." Heads bowed and Michelle prayed. Her prayer was a little longer than her previous cry of desperation. She thanked the Lord for the trip, the safety they had today, and the time of fellowship they were enjoying. She also asked that her words might be understandable and of some encouragement. Michelle looked up at the dimly lit faces and took a deep breath.

"Some of you don't know me too well, so I'd like to start with a little bit of background. I was not brought up a Protestant. My mother was Catholic and diligently brought us out to church. My parents did the best they could to teach me morals. My mom encouraged me to go to different Vacation Bible Schools throughout the summers. Even though she did not understand the simplicity of God's free gift, she felt the Bible was important. My four siblings and I put a lot of stress on my parent's marriage, but for the most part we were good kids who stayed out of trouble. I, however, was a very stubborn child who gave my mom much grief. My mother tried so hard to teach me the finer points of being a female, but I refused all her home economic lessons of cooking, cleaning, laundry, and so on. Whenever she tried to teach me something feminine, I would run out of the house and busy myself in my dad's woodshop.

"Even though I was a source of grief for my mom, I knew that my parents loved me, because I could see their love for us. Their smiles, laughter, and sacrifices were huge; they joyfully did things for us. My mom would go out of her way to give us what she never had as a kid. I am very fortunate to have the parents I do. I didn't fully appreciate all they did for me until after I was on my own and got saved. Even though their love for us was evident in their actions, they spent way too much time catering to us kids and not enough time on each other. They missed out on joyfully doing things for each other.

"I learned a lot of good things from my folks, but somewhere along the line I picked up a bad attitude toward marriage. When I moved out on my own, I determined not to let a man ruin my independence. At age eighteen, I bought my own house and was well on the way to running my own life. At age nineteen, my plans hit a snag.

"I started attending a Bible study. The scriptures I learned there forced me to see my sin nature. I was confronted with a choice. To either acknowledge God's Word as true or to justify my sins. I chose to take God at His word. My hideous sin nature loomed over me like a dark cloud. The Bible says, 'the wages of sin is death.' I knew I deserved hell. My sins had been more inward and hidden, but yet I knew God saw them.

"The Scriptures also say, 'for by grace are you saved through faith, and that not of yourselves; it is the gift of God, not of works least any man should boast.' My previous religion and good deeds could not earn eternal life for me. God was not impressed by my fake outward appearance. The only thing that would impress God would be Him seeing His Son in me. I saw that 'Christ Jesus came into the world to save sinners.' That God had shown His love to me, in that while I was yet sinfully gross, Christ died for me. I could be made holy through the offering of the body of Jesus Christ once for all. I did what Acts 16:31 said to: 'Believe on the Lord Jesus Christ and thou shalt be saved.' My faith was transferred from myself, my religious works, my good deeds; and instead, my faith was put in the Lord Jesus Christ, in His perfect payment for sin. My faith rested in the simple belief that He died for me, was buried, and rose again the third day. I accepted the free gift of eternal life.

"John 10:28 was a wonderful reminder of my eternal security in Christ. 'And I give unto them eternal life and they shall never perish, neither shall any man pluck them out of my hand.' And 1 John 3:13 gave me the assurance that my previous religion could not guarantee. 'These things have I written unto you that believe on the name of the Son of God that ye may know that you have eternal life, and that ye may believe on the name of the Son of God.'

"At nineteen years of age, the whole course of my life changed direction. The more I attended Bible studies, the more my faith grew, and I knew I could trust Christ to manage my life. I didn't, however, give Him control of everything. One thing that I refused to surrender was my attitude toward marriage. I could not relinquish my "man-pleasing" department. I was determined not to please a man. Not any man. I would not bend over backwards for any of the male species.

"If a man was going to like me, it was going to be for who I was inside, not what I looked like on the outside. This wasn't all bad. It kept me from getting all decked up to snag a guy. Instead, my baggy, tomboyish clothes made any prospective mate dig deeper than skin. I took Proverbs 31:30 a bit too far. 'Favor is deceitful and beauty is vain; but a woman that feareth the Lord, she shall be praised.' I put all the emphasis on the hidden man of the heart with no thought to the exterior. With that type of attitude, it's a miracle I'm even married.

"When we were dating, I didn't try to look nice for Jerry. I was who I was. After we were married, I was just thrilled that he liked me for who I was. I took 1 Peter 3:3–4 and really stretched it. 'Whose adorning let it not be that outward adorning of plaiting the hair, and of wearing of gold, or putting on of apparel: but let it be the hidden man of the heart, in that which is not corruptible, even the ornament of a meek and quiet spirit, which is in the sight of God of great price.'

"I hardly ever bothered to dress up. On Sundays, Jerry would drop little hints that he would like to see me in a dress. I always had an excuse not to wear one; it was either too hot or too cold or we were going to someone's house after the service and I didn't want to be stuck wearing a dress all day. I always sensed a hurt in Jerry when he heard my excuses; but those thoughts were quickly dismissed and I moved on. My ammunition verses were always loaded in my mind ready to justify my actions.

"God, however, was throwing a different verse at me. First Corinthians 7:34: 'There is a difference also between a wife and a virgin. The unmarried woman careth for the things of the Lord, that she may be holy both in body and in spirit: but she that is married careth for the things of the world, how she may please her husband.' I ignored this verse and all its implications. I was not going to please Jerry, and that was it; or so I thought. My little world was shaken two years into our marriage. I was the matron of honor at my friend, Rosanne's, wedding. She had an ideal fairytale wedding pictured in her mind. Rosanne wanted me and her bridesmaid to look the part. Goldilocks is what I ended up looking like. Nonetheless, DJ's mom, Ruth, was the hairstylist for the big event. I was not given an option of how or if I wanted my hair done. I didn't have a choice.

"I was pretty uncomfortable about the whole situation. My face turned red, I bit my tongue, and I sat down for my turn. Ruth could tell how awful I felt. I was so embarrassed by all the attention my hair was getting. She was calm and professional and did the best she could to doll me up. My husband later told me that was the prettiest he had ever seen me, and he couldn't quit gawking at me. His comment and a remark Ruth made to me ended up haunting me for years. When Ruth was doing my hair, she tried to encourage me but only ended up troubling me. She said, 'Why don't you want to look nice? Don't you want your husband to look at you, or would you rather that he looked at other women. If you don't give him something to look at, he will look elsewhere.'"

"*Ouch*!" A couple ladies simultaneously interjected.

"Yeah, that's how I felt. Just like I got slapped in the face. At first I was upset. I thought, *How could she say such a thing? She doesn't really know Jerry. He loves me for who I am; he would never look at another woman.* I thought, *I'm just going to have to prove her wrong.* For years after that, I secretly observed my husband whenever we were in the presence of shapely women. I did not like the results of my observations. Ruth obviously knew what she was talking about.

"Even with that knowledge, I still fought the truth for years. I did not want to please my husband. Not only did that attitude affect the way I dressed, but it also spilled over into how I cooked, cleaned house, and so on. My hair would stand up on end if he gave me any suggestions of how he would like things. If he hinted at lasagna for supper, I fed him spaghetti. If he mentioned that he liked the bed made in the morning, I told him 'Do it yourself, baby.' My pride and independent spirit hated being told what to do. I know it really wasn't Jerry I was wrestling with, it was God. Jerry was the only one I could take it out on.

"Several months ago I received a phone call from a lady. She was struggling in her marriage and shared some difficulties with me. She was very cautious not to bash her husband, but I could sense through the sad phone call that some of her struggles stemmed from her husband's limited vocabulary. Because this man never used the words *please, thank you, I'm sorry,* or *I love you*, he came off as being very demanding. His demanding nature lacked the tenderness his wife so craved. She never heard those three little words that used to come so easily when they were dating. A big question mark always remained in her head. 'Does he love me anymore?'

"The conversation was overwhelming, but when I got off the phone, I was rejoicing in the sweet, kind, and tender man God had provided for me. Jerry is not demanding or unfeeling. He isn't the type to make me a hunting widow for months on end. He's sensitive and much too nice. I don't deserve him. He's not difficult to be around.

"This realization hit me so hard. I was faced with how much my husband joyfully does for me. With the phone still in my hand, I prayed and thanked God for my husband. I was reminded of how much I loved this man but yet of how little I showed it. I held back a lot from him. God had my attention. Forcing myself to continue the prayer, I asked God, 'How can I show Jerry that I love him?' In that still small voice, He replied and said, 'You can start by dressing up for him more often.' My instant argument was truthful in that I could not afford to buy nice clothes. God already knew that, but His loving rebuke showed me that I had never prayed and asked Him for better clothes. I was ashamed of my lack of faith, but my prayer continued, and I requested clothes that might please my husband.

"God also showed me other little inexpensive treasures of love that I could bestow on my man. Smiles were free, and I could wear one more often. A clean house to welcome my work-weary husband would also require no money, just time. Food was also a good way to his heart. Having a nice supper ready could say I love you more powerfully than the actual words. God showed me a lot of other little things that I had been negligent to see and act on. I started to get Shayla dressed up in nice outfits to welcome her daddy home. Pretty soon she was dressing up on her own. She wanted to please Daddy. The more little things I did that God had shown me, the easier it became to smile. I was wearing a smile because I really meant it. It wasn't forced; it was a result of doing things joyfully out of love.

"Within days of praying for nice clothes, a little old lady gave me a couple bags of shirts she no longer wore. They weren't fancy, but they were definitely more feminine than anything I had in my closet. Then my mom passed on to me some pants she no longer fit into. Again, they were not what I would have picked out, but I rejoiced in knowing they were from the Lord. After a while I was able to obtain some new clothes on sale. A new nightie was included in that purchase. I had never owned a nightie before. I had to, however, overcome the awful feeling that I was wearing a dress eight hours every day.

"To look nice for my husband was important. God wanted to drive this point home just a little harder. My friend, Joan, lent me the book, *For Women Only*, by Shaunti Feldhahn. I read it purposely when Jerry was gone camping. I struggled with what I read, and when my husband returned from his trip, I had lots of questions to ask him. I needed to know if the book accurately described him. The book touched on how men have the mind of a Rolodex file system. They only have to see a shapely figure once to have the image burned into their mind forever. That image could pop up without notice or be conjured up at any time. Men are overwhelmed with the visual stimuli they receive everyday. They can't go anywhere without seeing an underdressed woman. The grocery store, work, driving downtown, the gas station, even in the supposed safe haven of church women flaunt their bodies and men notice. Jerry said he doesn't want to always be looking at women; he would rather look away, choosing to honor me. He was very honest in admitting that this is a problem for him. He said he had to memorize Job 31:1 to help combat this dilemma, 'I made a covenant with mine eyes; why then should I think upon a maid?' Jerry wanted to know if other men struggled with this too. Whenever Jerry had occasion to be with other Christian men, he would watch them to see what they did in the presence of beautiful women. He immediately perceived the same struggle in them. He wasn't trying to justify his lust problem, but he did admit that it was a huge area of weakness for him. One in which he needed God's help daily.

"One place a husband should feel safe to 'sneak peeks' is in the home. It's OK for a man to look at his wife, but do we give our husbands anything to look at? Not that we have to walk around wearing a skimpy bikini, but do our husbands like how we dress? Do they like our clothes? Are we sensitive to their needs? Are we willing to please them with our nighttime attire? Do they have something to look forward to seeing at home? Are we encouraging them to honor us?"

"Oh my," declared Karen. "Is that why my husband asks me, 'Don't you have anything more feminine to wear to bed?' I just prance around the house in my boxers and baggy T-shirts and don't think anything of it. I don't even own a nightie."

Michelle added, "It's taken me nine years of marriage to see this truth, but more than anything, I need to diligently pray for my husband, particularly in this area of weakness. If Job, the great man of God, struggled with what he saw and had to make a covenant with his eyes, how much more do our husbands in this day and age struggle? Our men need our prayers and understanding."

Someone else spoke up. "Michelle, you mentioned that church should be a safe haven for our men, but it isn't. How do you tell a church lady that married men are looking at her or that she's a stumbling block to a faithfully married man's worship?"

"That's a good question. I know Pastor has addressed the issue quite frankly in church, but he can't force anyone to change. I just remember how naïve I was as a young person, and I have to wonder if the younger ladies are oblivious to the fact of how men really think. They probably have no idea that the tight-fitting clothes, short skirts, and immodest shirts that reveal their belly and bust, have ruined many worship services for the men. Such ladies that sing specials have often discouraged Jerry. He gets frustrated when he has to look at his shoes rather than the singers. Church is the last place he should be bombarded by these images. If a lady is naïve but has a soft heart, I would encourage her to read

Shaunti's book. The bold, direct approach may be necessary in some cases. Being prayerful should be the first step."

The discussion continued on in a lively fashion. Each woman added her thoughts to the difficult and emotional topic. Much later, the yawns that had been suppressed, surfaced. Annie and Michelle bid the others good night and headed for their own tent.

CHAPTER THIRTEEN

A GOOD NIGHT'S SLEEP

The mosquitoes that previously swarmed the ladies had vanished. The night was visibly chilly. Michelle's breath hung suspended in mid-air. She couldn't wait to get into the tent and crawl into her cozy sleeping bag. She hoped, with the relieved stress of her devotion off of her mind, she would get a good night's slumber. Her shoulders ached from the canoe yolk that dug into her earlier. She missed Jerry and the shoulder rub he would not be giving her tonight.

Once situated inside, getting comfortable was harder than she thought it would be. "Annie, could I bother you for a shoulder rub? The canoes were not nice to me today."

"Sure. I once took a class to learn how to give massages. It was really helpful."

Michelle was not disappointed in the results of Annie's class. It was relaxing. "Jerry would just love it if I took a class like that," Michelle said in the same breath as a yawn. "Thank you." She was relaxed enough and tired enough she actually thought she might fall asleep. Falling asleep on a camping trip would be a miracle. She never slept well on camping trips, especially when her protector was not with her. She crawled into her bag. Her left hand held her headlamp, and that is where the light would conveniently stay for the night. The other reached to feel the proximity of the hatchet she placed near her bedroll. Feeling it to be there, the empty hand retreated into the warmth of the bag. If something was going to attack her tent, looking for a meal, she was not going to just roll over and be dinner. She would put up a fight.

Michelle lay on her back listening to the stillness of the night. There was a frog outside jumping onto the tent wall. She knew that to be a non-threatening sound. She listened more carefully and was content not to hear the cracking-branch sound. Knowing her nighttime camping fears might over rule her sound mind and tired body, Michelle put up a silent prayer.

"Michelle, are you still awake?" Annie whispered.

"Yes."

"I'm glad I got to be in the same canoe and tent as you."

"Why?"

"I feel safe with you."

Michelle chuckled. "You probably feel safe because we have the hatchet in our tent and the others don't." She did not have the courage to tell Annie of her worrisome fears that threatened to rob her of all sleep.

"No, it's just that you're so experienced and you know what you're doing out here. If you weren't here, none of us would survive. I wouldn't know how to do anything. If I was with Mike, he would do everything and I wouldn't bother to learn for myself. You're encouraging us to learn. Thanks for putting this trip together."

"No problem, Annie. I'm really glad you could come. And to be honest, being in the same tent and canoe with you has been an answer to prayer."

Michelle wanted to visit more, but Annie's talkative streak was over. A longer conversation would have distracted Michelle from her worrying. Instead of counting sheep, Michelle decided to count blessings. She was just thanking the Lord for the safety and how the trip had gone so far. That's when she heard a noise outside.

The other tent zipped open and shut. DJ and Jenna walked by and went to the latrine. *No big deal,* thought Michelle, *they're just making a potty run.* Their time at the latrine took longer than Michelle thought it should. Eventually they made it back to their own tent, and Michelle started to drift off to sleep. Moments later, she was awakened by the same ladies once again running to the latrine. Michelle panicked and sat up. Something was wrong. She waited for them to return, and asked, "Is everything OK?"

"No. Both DJ and I have diarrhea, but DJ thinks she's going to throw up. Is there anything she can use in the tent?"

"There should be a cooking pot by the mess kit." Silently they left for the tent.

Michelle was not sure how worried she should be, but she was definitely concerned. Her worry greatly increased as Jenna and DJ's trips to the latrine grew in number. On one of the trips, she whispered to the passersbys, "Any idea what the problem might be from?"

"DJ's not sure, but mine might have something to do with all the berries I ate today. All the sugary sweets probably didn't help either." Earlier, Jenna thought that perhaps the lake water had been the culprit. She dismissed that thought when her mom, Michelle, and Annie remained unaffected.

The ladies in Jenna's tent made a pact with each other earlier in the day. They determined that no one should go to the latrine alone at night. The buddy system gave them a sense of security. DJ, in her dire condition, was too rushed to worry about the buddy system. When she felt the urge, she rushed out, neglecting to alert her buddy. Jenna, still not feeling 100 percent, slept lightly and noticed when DJ left. She was always about thirty seconds behind her friend, not wanting her to be alone. The potty parade continued all night.

Annie slept through it, but Michelle could not find sleep. Her worrywarts were growing fast. *What if DJ has heat stroke or needs to be rushed to the hospital?* The wheels in Michelle's head were turning. She was the leader and would have to take responsibility if any action was needed. A plan was formulating in her mind. She was determined that if DJ were dying, she would wake up Annie. Both she and Annie would strap on headlamps, put Michelle's Thermarest mattress on the canoe bottom, lay DJ in the canoe, and cover her with a sleeping bag. Annie and she would paddle like crazy. If DJ were too ill to walk across the portage, Michelle would have to make two trips across, one with the canoe and the other carrying DJ. If DJ were more than Michelle could manage, Annie would have to pitch in with the load.

Jenna and Karen would have to fend for themselves at camp and wait for Michelle to get back from the hospital. Michelle felt that neither lady would be able to successfully break camp and portage everything that was left. They would just have to wait. Michelle did not like the thought of canoeing at night. She prayed that daylight would come quickly.

DJ was not having fun and wanted to get out of the woods—now. Her tent mates calmed her down and convinced her to take an aspirin. DJ was known to get excited about trips and work her nerves up into knots. She usually ended up sick the first night into any trip. Had Michelle known that fact, she might have been spared some extra worrying. DJ and Jenna fell asleep shortly before dawn.

With a dim light illuminating the sky, Michelle listened to Annie's soft breathing and eventually fell asleep herself. Her sleep was short but adequate. Michelle would have to rely on God and adrenaline for any possible drain of endurance. She had caught less than an hour of sleep when the bright sunshine finally woke her. The sunshine was intense. Michelle sat up in her bag and could feel the day was going to be hot. Her Bible lay next to the hatchet. She reached for the book and enjoyed some quiet time reading and praying as Annie slept on.

Michelle left the tent a little nervous about what condition she might find DJ in. At least the sun was shining and her nighttime fears were set aside. With the sun shining, she felt as though she could face anything. All was quiet. Taking her camp chair, she went to the kitchen and set up her seat on one of the logs. She relaxed and soaked up as much of the view as she could.

She could only sit still for so long. It was not her nature to sit. At home, she put the verse, Psalm 46:10, "Be still and know that I am God," on her wall to remind her it was OK to be still. Recently, Shayla had seen a picture of Michelle sitting in a recliner with Levi and Caden snuggled on her lap, all tucked under a blanket. The little girl asked, "Mom, what was wrong with you, were you on bed rest?" Shayla was not accustomed to seeing her mother relax.

The next step of action formulated in her mind. She followed the dictates of her growling stomach. Karen was up now and so was Annie. The three of them lowered the food pack with ease. Michelle opened the cooler bucket and felt inside; she was relieved it was still cold. The chilly night did much to preserve the freshness of the eggs. Cheesy omelets were on this morning's menu. Michelle was counting on hungry campers. She had cracked eighteen eggs for this meal. The omelets were mixed together at home and then frozen in a Ziploc bag. Now all she had to do was make sure they did not burn to the pan.

The eggs were cooked to perfection. Only Karen, Annie, and Michelle were up to enjoy them. Michelle was not going to wake the other two women. The longer they slept, the better Michelle would feel about the day's prognoses. The three ate as much as they could but hardly put a dent in the eggs. The remaining eggs were left sitting in the pan. Karen was in a talkative mood and that was good. Neither Michelle nor Annie had known Karen prior to the trip. They took this opportunity to get to know her.

CHAPTER FOURTEEN

MOTHER AND DAUGHTER

Karen stared at the bare ground between her feet. After a moment of thoughtfulness, she spoke. "I've been admiring the landscaping around here, it's just beautiful, ya know. At first, I wondered, how it could be better? How would I change it? But this campsite's got a rugged beauty all its own. There's even natural rock steps leading down to our tent site. I just love how the kitchen is on one level, our tent bedroom is on the lower level, and the shoreline is like basement level. It's so cool how it's laid out. Ya know, I don't think I would add or change a single thing. God did a pretty good job in the first place." Both Annie and Michelle agreed.

"Don't you just love this view?" Karen continued as she looked out over the lake. "When I'm at home, I'm always outside. Mostly, I love dinging around with my flowers and landscaping. At one of the places that Jenna and I lived, we stuck a small fortune into landscaping the place. We had a lot of fun doing it, but before we moved, the landlord made us undo everything we did. I couldn't believe he made us take it apart. It had really dressed the place up and added value. It wasn't no sloppy haphazard job either."

"So you took everything apart?" Annie inquired.

"We had to or we wouldn't get our damage deposit back. We ended up giving away all our expensive landscaping materials to various neighbors. We couldn't take it with us."

The forty-five-year-old sandy-haired mother was mind boggling to Michelle. When she first learned that Jenna's mom was coming on the trip, Michelle instantly warmed to the idea of having an older mother figure with them, one that would watch over and pamper them. After meeting Karen yesterday, Michelle had to change her mental image of the mother. Karen did not fit the picture in her mind. Jenna's mother was spontaneous and carefree. She acted younger than her twenty-three-year-old daughter. Karen's carefree style camouflaged her rough past.

Michelle was remembering something she heard earlier and asked, "Did I hear correctly that you had been diagnosed with leukemia?"

"Yeah, I've had three bouts with the disease. I'm currently in remission. Thanks to my brother, Johnny, I was able to have a bone marrow transplant. I feel pretty good right now. I do get a bit winded at times. I quit smoking a few months ago and am slowly getting some of my stamina back. This camping trip is going to either make me or break me. If I can survive this experience, I hope to do more hiking when I get home. It'd be a real shame to let this exercise go to waste. But yeah, God has really used this leukemia to get my attention."

"Do you have peace with God and an assurance of where you will spend your eternity?" asked Michelle.

"Yeah, but this faith stuff is all pretty new to me. My daughter is actually responsible for leading me to Christ. I haven't exactly been the greatest mom in the world. As a matter of fact, I've been downright selfish. I really put Jenna through a lot. I would get involved with my party pals and sorta just vanish. Jenna was tossed like a rag doll from one foster home to the next. After a while, I'd get my act together and Jenna would move back in with me. When she was about thirteen, I disappeared again. This time I ended up in Alaska and Jenna in another foster home.

"I hated myself for what I did to my daughter. My time in Alaska was miserable; all I could see was my daughter's smiling face. When I returned from Alaska, Jenna moved back in with me. She always forgave me and moved on with life. She never resented me or acted bitter toward me. She had such a forgiving spirit. She could of really stuck it to me, ya know.

"To this day, I still don't know much about raising kids; I missed out on Jenna's childhood. When other moms talk about kid issues, I can't relate at all. I'm not proud of my past." Karen paused. Annie and Michelle waited silently, not knowing if there was more.

"Jenna was bubbly and forgiving before, but when she met Rory, got married, and started going to Bible studies, then there was a real big spark in her eyes. She was so soft to God's spirit, ya know. I wanted what she had. I saw a peace in her life that I knew I didn't have. Jenna kept talking to me about Jesus, but it just wasn't clicking. She didn't give up on me. She was persistent; and eventually it clicked.

"I don't know much about the Bible, but I want to know more. I've got a hunger deep down that wants the truth of God's Word. My work schedule is hectic at the restaurant on the weekends. I should just ask my boss for time off on Sundays and see what happens."

At this time Michelle interjected her thoughts into Karen's pause. "Attending a good Bible-believing church is pretty important. God says not to forsake the assembling of yourselves together with those of like precious faith. Our faith will grow as we hear God's Word taught. Frankly, it's nice to be able to fellowship and bounce things off of other believers. They make for good sounding boards."

"Yeah, I know I need to get out to church more."

Karen chatted a bit longer, all the while showing a deep respect and admiration for her daughter's faith, which was now her own. Both Annie and Michelle enjoyed their visit with Karen. While learning about her, they also got to know Jenna better.

Jenna was relatively new to the assembly of the Grace Bible Church. She and Rory moved to the Iron Range from the cities only two years prior. Michelle was hoping for a chance to visit with Jenna and to get better acquainted, but for now, she wanted to ask Karen more questions. DJ chose that moment to make her appearance in the land of the living. At the sight of her, Michelle was distracted and lost her train of thought.

"How are you feeling?" Michelle inquired as DJ rubbed the sleep from her eyes.

"I've been better, but I think I will live."

"I cooked up a whole mess of eggs. Are you hungry?"

DJ looked at the eggs and felt her stomach turn. "I better not try to eat right now."

"Well, at least force yourself to drink. The temperature is climbing fast."

DJ heeded Michelle's suggestion and helped herself to a cup of Tang and decided a granola bar would be safe to try. Jenna emerged from her lower level bedroom and eyed the eggs. She was hungry and scooped herself a small plateful. Jenna thanked the Lord for the nourishment but felt sick when she saw the bacon. She loved bacon, but for some reason it made her want to throw up this morning. *I wonder if I'm pregnant?* As quickly as the thought entered her mind, she also dismissed it. She forced herself to eat the small helping on her plate. She wanted to eat more but couldn't.

Michelle sighed as she looked at the leftover eggs. *I wonder if seagulls are cannibalistic? Maybe,* she silently pondered. "Annie, would you mind going with me to visit our neighbors? I want to bring them some more goodies. The pan needs to be emptied before doing dishes."

Annie watched Michelle light the burner and put a pan of water on to warm. "Is it OK if I do the dishes this morning?" asked Annie.

"Sure, no skin off my back."

The leftover eggs were quickly paddled over to the little island and deposited. The hotdogs had not been appreciated. Annie efficiently removed them. Paddling back to camp, Michelle remembered that more drinking water needed to be pumped.

By the time the ladies returned, the dishwater was ready. Annie took over the little kitchen and tidied up. Then she and DJ left to explore another neighboring island. Karen was in the tent trying to catch up on some lost sleep, while Jenna situated herself on a granite ledge overlooking the lake with her Bible. She volunteered to do tonight's devotion and was now immersing herself in God's Word in preparation for the task.

Once her thoughts were wrapped up for the devotion, she let her mind wander. She soaked up the beautiful view in front of her and wished her husband were here to share it with her. She smiled as she thought about how eager he had been for her to go on this trip. She was fortunate to be camping. Had Rory even raised an eyebrow over her going, she would have dropped the trip faster than a dead mouse. Despite her rough night, she was enjoying herself.

Preparing for this trip had been fairly easy. Michelle had taken on all the planning and left nothing for Jenna to plan, other than her devotion. Jenna loved to plan things. All her concentrated efforts would have been poured into planning the trip had Michelle not done so. She would have scheduled every minute of the day with meaningful activity. Nothing would have been left to chance. Jenna was either a hot or cold type of person. When it came to planning an event, she was hot; her whole heart was in it. She often clashed with her more laidback friends. "Just let things happen the way they happen," she was often told.

Jenna sighed and admitted to herself that even if she would have had the responsibility she wouldn't have known how to plan for this trip. She had never been into the Boundary Waters before. Now that she had, and knew a little more what to expect, she would be sure to set up a trip for Rory and herself.

Jenna looked off to her right and saw Michelle doing the lazy fisherman-thing off of the same rock bluff as she. Michelle was reclining in her chair with a book in one hand and her pole by her side. Occasionally she would look down and check on her motionless bobber.

Michelle was staring at her book, but the words were not registering. She did not come on this trip to read. She came with the hopes of getting to know these ladies better. If she allowed herself to be absorbed into the novel, she would shut the world out until the book was read cover to cover. The fishing pole was a worthy distraction. Even at that, she dared not hope for a large fish to find her hook. Knowing how shallow the lake was, she doubted the existence of big fish in this lake.

Michelle put the book down, reeled in her line, and cast it in a different direction. She was pleasantly surprised to see Jenna walk her way and sit down.

"Anything biting?"

"Nothing. How are you feeling? Are you OK from last night?"

"I feel OK. A little tired, though. I'll try to get a nap in before lunch. The ledge I was just on would be the perfect spot to nap and catch some sun too."

"I haven't heard, are you still working at the bank?"

"No. It's a credit union."

"Isn't that the same as a bank?"

"No, there's a big difference."

Jenna quickly brought Michelle up to speed on the fundamental differences between the two institutions. As Jenna talked about work, there was an uncertain look in Jenna's eyes that made Michelle ask, "Do you enjoy it?"

"The work is OK, but no, I don't enjoy it. More and more I just want to be at home. I want to be able to experiment in the kitchen. I love to cook, but by the time I get home from work, I'm drained and don't feel like cooking. I would just love to have the flexibility to have lots of dinner guests and to make fancy meals for them. I love having company over."

"What else would you do at home?"

"I'd do more gardening too. Mostly, I just want to be a mother. Even though I don't have kids of my own, I'm sure we will someday soon." Jenna's thoughts drifted to the unpleasant memories of two miscarriages. She quickly snapped out of those thoughts, not giving the memory a chance to fester. "Did you know we are house hunting?"

"No. How is it going?"

"It's hard finding a decent house in the price range we can afford. We are confident, though, that God will lead us to the right one."

"What area of the Iron Range are you looking in?"

"All over. We haven't narrowed it down yet."

"Well, now I can pray about something specific for you. A house."

"Thanks."

The conversation continued. After a while, they decided to go explore the same island from which DJ and Annie had just returned.

Once back at camp, Michelle remembered the chore she forgot to do. Looking around for anyone idle, she spotted Annie. "Would you mind manning the canoe while I pump our drinking water?"

"That would be fine, let me find my life jacket."

CHAPTER FIFTEEN

TRUCK ENGINES AND SCORPIONS

In order to keep the water filter from plugging up with sediment, Michelle preferred to pump from a canoe, rather than off the shore. In this murky lake, Michelle soon discovered her location made no difference. The filter clogged quickly and pumping grew slow and hard. Michelle was wearing herself out as she struggled with the pump. She still managed to visit as she worked. More of her effort was channeled into the pump rather than conversation. Annie took over and gave Michelle's arm a break.

Michelle's focus changed and her tongue made up for her idle hands as she watched Annie work with the defiant pump. "I've got a new name for you."

"Oh yeah, what is it?" Annie curiously asked, looking up at Michelle.

"Duramax."

"Dura what?"

"Duramax. It's the diesel engine in a Chevy truck."

"Why would you nickname me after a truck engine?"

"The name represents a real workhorse of an engine. The Duramax diesel is quiet and powerful. It does its job with class."

"I still don't get the connection."

"In case you haven't noticed, you've been my slave. Every chore I've thrown at you, you do it quickly and quietly. You don't mumble or shirk. Not only are you quiet like the Duramax, you're also stronger than you appear. You've got the strength of endurance to keep on trucking. You're a pretty good little workhorse. My husband will be eating his words when I tell him about Duramax. He said you were a wimpy woman."

Annie's brown and green eyes, looking browner than green at the moment, twinkled with amusement. "If I tell Mike what you just told me, he would never believe me."

"Well, maybe I'll have to introduce him to Duramax," Michelle said with a teasing smile.

Annie shook her head and laughed as she resumed pumping. Silence followed as Michelle's mood turned more serious. The sound of the dripping water falling into the jug held the attention of the ladies. Michelle broke the water's trance after a minute of silence. "The first lake we canoed across yesterday is where Carmen's cabin is. That's the place I've reserved in case the weather turns on us."

"What's the place like?"

"Oh, it's beautiful. The log cabin is cedar and fairly new. It was built in 2001. The builders trucked everything across the ice in the winter to build it. The cabin itself is small and cozy. It's only one room, but all the windows make it seem larger. Every window you look out of, you see lake.

"Carmen is an artist, and she's done a wonderful job decorating the interior. Her artistic touch has turned an old tree stump into a table, a beaver chewed piece of driftwood into a coat rack, and little sticks, stones, feathers, and pinecones into a beautiful border on an old mirror. She painted the heat shield behind the wood stove to look like the woods on a foggy morning. She's got a great eye for detail. Being inside the cabin feels the same as being outside. I built two log beds for her that sit along one wall divided only by the door. Two more trundle beds hide under the log ones.

"There's no kitchen. All the cooking is done outside. The latrine is about one hundred feet away from the cabin, hidden away in the underbrush. You can only get to the cabin by water, there's no road. When you approach the property from the lake, the beach is pure rolling granite. There's no need for a dock; boats can simply glide onto the shore. Walking the path to the cabin is almost magical. You feel like you've just entered a fairytale. The property is on a point that juts out into the lake. It's also got a fantastic little area away from the cabin where you can pitch a tent and feel like you're out in the middle of nowhere.

"Annie, I want you to see this place so bad. You would just love it. If the weather holds up, and we don't need to use it, maybe on our way out of the woods we can stop at the cabin and have lunch or something. I love going there. It's so relaxing."

Annie's curiosity was aroused. "How did you discover this place?"

"Carmen is a neighbor of ours. I do little projects for her in exchange for the use of her cabin. The trade works pretty well. If I didn't do this, Jerry and I would never take a vacation. I plan it all and simply tell Jerry he's going on vacation. He mumbles and grumbles 'cause he hates taking the time off from work, but once he's out here and gets a fishing rod in his hand, he enjoys himself. I've got a trip planned for Labor Day weekend with a babysitter all lined up for the kids. I can't wait to go."

Michelle's words ran out as she watched Annie concentrate on filling the last water jug. She was imaging the relaxing time she would have over Labor Day weekend. The intense sun brought her mind reeling back to the present. The sweat was rolling off both women, especially Annie. The temperature was climbing fast and showed no sign of stopping. *Today would be a perfect day to get heat stroke,* worried Michelle. "We better get this water back to the ladies."

Duramax agreed and quickly began paddling. They traveled in silence, each in their own little world.

DJ greeted the canoeists as they approached the shore, but her attention was not on them. She was intently studying the ground, looking for something. "I can't figure out where the buzzing sound is coming from. It almost sounds as if it's coming from by my feet."

Michelle heard the buzzing as well and scanned the immediate area to see if the sound belonged to threatening insects with stingers. "DJ, all I see flying around are the black flies. I hardly think they're anything to worry about."

"I'm pretty sure they are bees, and there's one flying around my head now. *Ooooh!* I can hear it! I hate bees!" DJ's eyes were squinted shut, both pointer fingers thrust into her ears as squeals of fear escaped her mouth to drown out the buzzing, and she was jumping around like she was on fire.

Michelle was greatly amused by her friend's antics. She wanted to laugh but thought she might appear too cold-hearted and cruel. She restrained herself. The black fly Michelle saw buzzing around DJ's head left the area, and DJ opened her eyes to find Michelle's muffled expression fixed upon her. "I'm sorry. I am afraid of bees. I can't help it."

Michelle did not try convincing DJ that she had mistakenly identified the insect. Nor did she try to warn that had it actually been a bee it was best to be still and not dance around like a chicken with its head cut off.

Insects usually did not bother the California Kid. Having been homeschooled in the desert region of the state, DJ was used to having frozen locusts, scorpions, tarantulas, and other assorted animals in her parent's freezer. On one occasion, her science experiment, a frozen scorpion, slowly inched its way off the examining plate, much to the young scientist's surprise. It had not been frozen long enough to die. The scorpion was carefully replaced in the freezer and was left to sit too long. Upon the next examination, it simply shattered.

The two, carrying water jugs, left DJ to finish her examination of the shoreline. It was lunch time and sandwiches needed to be prepared. Michelle entered her tent first to put away a book. She lost her breath as the boiling, stale tent air hit her in the face. Michelle quickly retreated. She saw Jenna sitting on a kitchen log. "Is your mother still sleeping in your tent?"

"Yes. Why?"

"You might want to get her out of there. Your tent is probably just as hot as mine, and besides, it's time for lunch."

"All right, I'll go wake up Sleeping Beauty."

Moments later Karen, with Jenna next to her, emerged from the fabric sauna. Michelle handed Karen a water jug. "Thanks for getting me out of there; I didn't realize it was so hot. I could have died of dehydration. I guess I was almost like the frog in the pot of water that doesn't notice the increasing heat. The frog always dies in those experiments."

The group sat down to a simple lunch. Michelle thought twice about sitting on a kitchen log; instead she found a shady place on the ground and set up her chair. "Drink lots of water," Michelle reminded everyone again. She was driving the water bandwagon pretty hard; their lives depended on it.

The lunchtime conversation turned toward setting an agenda for the rest of the day. Michelle remained silent, not wanting to express her heart's desire. Karen, DJ, and Jenna wanted relaxation. The night had drained them. Annie was not saying much, so Michelle asked, "What would you like to do, Annie?"

Her response made Michelle's breath catch in her throat and her pulse increase. "I want to go to the cabin. Michelle, you've talked so much about this place that I've just got to experience it for myself. Besides we've done everything there is to do here."

Shy, timid Annie had an opinion and actually shared it. That shocked Michelle almost as much as the fact that Annie had voiced Michelle's secret desire. Michelle's mind was whirling. Annie was right; they had done everything there was to do here, so much so that the rest of the day seemed boring if they stayed here when there was a new adventure to be had. As the group leader, Michelle presented the facts so a choice could be made.

"If that was an option the rest of you would agree to, it would take us about an hour and a half to pack up and break camp. If we slowed our pace down so we wouldn't overdo it in the heat, we could be to the cabin by suppertime. There would be no chores of setting up tents, gathering firewood, or hanging the pack; we wouldn't have to be in a rush to get set up. The lake is beautifully clean and great for swimming, not as slimy either. The lake is deeper and probably houses a lot more fish than we're seeing here."

Annie's suggestion sprouted in the more relaxation-oriented ladies, and they soon embraced the thought of leisurely cabin life. Michelle's joy was evident as she raced around packing up the bulk of the gear. She was a tornado doing circles around the rest of the ladies. She let the others move at their own pace, not wanting to be pushy in the heat. Camp was packed up in almost exactly an hour and a half.

Before the ladies were allowed to enter their canoes, Michelle put her foot down. "I want everyone to get in the lake and totally immerse yourselves. I want every inch of you wet, and that includes your shoes and lifejackets and caps, everything that you'll be wearing." Nobody liked the idea of fighting with the slime. "In this heat, its best that moisture evaporates off your clothes rather than you," Michelle said as she led the way into the brown water. By her example the others followed, and much to their surprise, they were greatly refreshed. "When you start drying off, dip your hat into the lake and put it on your head, it'll help you keep cool as we paddle. Oh, and when we get to the rapids, be prepared to roll around in it."

Michelle for now was done being bossy. The ladies shoved off and headed to the first portage around the rapids. There was always a sense of sadness and loss whenever Michelle had to leave a campsite that had been her home, even if it was for only one night. The loss she now felt was nothing compared to the joy of what she knew lay ahead at the cabin.

As the Grumman traveled past the little island where the hot dogs had once been left for the seagulls, Karen chuckled and gave the big granite rock one last look. She had affectionately named it the "Hot Dog Rock." She wasn't sure why, but she knew the rock would stand out as a monument in her mind. It would always remind her of their slimy and adventurous swim. Years from now, she would have the Hot Dog Rock to remember and look back on as an enjoyable and pleasant time in her life. With a huge smile, she turned her gaze away from the island and focused on the Alumacraft ahead of them. Rice Lake was lost from sight as the two canoes entered the short stretch of river to the portage.

The little portage welcomed the ladies with ease. When everything was across, Michelle went to explore the shallow rapids. There were no spots of any depth to sit in, so Michelle decided to lie on her back in an inch of water that rushed over a granite slab. When her back was all wet, she rolled over onto her belly.

The mother/daughter team liked the idea and rolled around too. Michelle cautioned the ladies not to get water on their lips. This was beaver water; the Giardia bug could make a person extremely sick.

Michelle had a friend who became quite ill after swimming in beaver water. She contracted the bug by simply licking her wet lips. Michelle's warning was heeded almost to the point of paranoia. Jenna was thinking too hard, trying to remember if she licked her lips or not. After some pictures were taken, the group pushed off down the lazy river.

Noticing that her skin was crawling, Michelle looked down at her arms and gasped. Her skin and clothes were moving with little worms. She knew these bugs came from the rapids she had just rolled around in. Not wanting to alarm the others, she silently picked off the worms and flicked them in the river. The worms were more annoying than threatening. Michelle was glad Annie was sitting in the front and could not see her predicament.

The river and Pond Lake passed quickly; the 160-rod portage now stared them in the face. The ladies knew what to expect. They took their time in crossing. Nobody was in a hurry. When the portage was successfully completed, Michelle's anticipation of Rock Lake and the cabin made her want to jump out of her skin. She felt like a giddy little kid waiting for her parents to wake up on Christmas day just so she could open her gifts. In this instance, it was not her opening up the gift; she could not wait for the others to see the cabin.

CHAPTER SIXTEEN

THE CABIN

The muddy mouth of the portage spit Michelle's canoe out into the clean deep water of Rock Lake. Michelle forgot about how tired she was from the draining night; adrenaline propelled her forward and she paddled with a renewed sense of energy. Each stroke fueled by passion, each stroke bringing her closer to the place of her daydreams.

As a teenager in high school, Michelle doodled on her folders, tablets, and on the brown grocery-bag coverings that protected her textbooks. If she had spare time between classes, in study hall, or if the teacher's monotone voice threatened to put her to sleep, her artistic hands recreated scenes from her summer trips into the Boundary Waters.

When studies grew dull, she stared at her drawings, mentally transporting herself into the woods she loved. The teacher's voice would fade as the distinct call of the loon echoed in her little world. Her black-and-white doodles of tall evergreens took on a fresh balsamic odor and a thriving forest green color. The water always sparkled with the shimmering diamond look, and the simple drawing of a canoe with two passengers came to life. Her imaginary red canoe added a splash of color to her daydreams. Michelle, liking to be in control, placed herself in the stern directing the path of the canoe. She could almost feel the cool drops of water striking her face from her partner's clumsy attempt at paddling. Every little drawing told a story, complete with sound, smell, color, and feeling. Even the smoky campfire smell, clinging to her clothes, could be imagined. Just as quickly as she entered the dream, she could also exit and tune the monotone voice back in. She often frequented her wonder world; she was fortunate that her grades never suffered from her mental excursions.

Over twenty years later Michelle still daydreamed. She did not, however, let her mind dangerously wander all over the Boundary Waters; instead, she let it securely settle into a cozy log cabin just on the edge of the BWCA. It was to that location she now paddled. The nomadic tent life still had appeal to Michelle, but the safety that the four solid walls offered was more alluring. A door that locked, walls that did not sway in the wind, and a roof that did not leak would allow her peace of mind and the sleep that a tent would not. Michelle longed for sleep tonight.

Annie's excited voice broke Michelle's silent reverie. She was pointing to the right at the rocky crag that jutted into the water. Eagles were circling above the pine trees that majestically sat on the granite rocks. On a little island to the left, several more bald eagles were perched in the tiptop limbs of a white pine stand. Both ladies paddled in silent awe of the great birds. Michelle thought it was weird to see the nine or ten eagles all gathered in one area flying back and forth. She wasn't complaining. As the eagles suspiciously watched them from above, Michelle had the odd sensation that she was intruding. She forced herself to paddle on.

The Grumman passengers felt more at ease to stop and indulge their eyes in the air show. When DJ tired of the eagles, she took advantage of the distraction. She grabbed her pole and opened the worm container, releasing the smell of death to invade her space. The bloated worms lay motionlessly on top of the drenched soil. Hoping that the fish were not fussy, DJ baited up her hook with one of the dead, smelly worms. She cast the line into the water and handed the pole to Karen who was duffing. Even though she was paddling, DJ was determined to do some trolling on the way to the cabin. She bought the worms for a purpose; she wanted a fish meal.

"Do you have to fish now?" asked Jenna. "Your line is getting in the way of my paddle." Sitting in the stern, she was trying to figure out how to maneuver the canoe without tangling up DJ's line.

Karen felt trapped in the middle and just held the rod, not knowing if she should reel it in or not.

"Just paddle on the other side of the canoe," retorted the determined fisherwoman. "I want fresh fish."

"I'll be surprised if she catches anything," Michelle said quietly to Annie. "She's got about an hour to try, though. If I wasn't in such a hurry to get to the cabin, I might try trolling myself. I can't wait for you to see the place. Thanks for convincing everyone to go."

"If you wanted to go to the cabin so bad, why didn't you say so? How come you kept quiet?"

"I knew how much DJ had her heart set on doing a Boundary Waters trip. I didn't want to disappoint her by cutting it short."

"Why was her heart so set on the Boundary Waters?"

"Her husband didn't think she could handle the BW. I think she had a point to prove."

"Oh. So when he finds out that we went to the cabin, he might say I told you so."

"I think you hit the nail on the head, Annie. Even my husband gave me a hard time when he learned about my backup plan. He was really upset about it."

"Why?"

"I don't think he wanted me to go to the cabin without him. He enjoys it there as well. He did say,

'If you're going into the BWCA, stick to the BWCA. Don't switch gears.' I did level with him beforehand and told him, 'You got to go on your trip and do the things you wanted to, now let me go on my trip and do the things I want to. It's my vacation.'"

"So is Jerry going to give you a hard time when you get back?"

"I don't know, but I'm not worried about it. I don't feel like I have to prove anything to him."

Michelle threw all her concentration into her paddle. The choppy waves made the ladies earn their mileage. The hour-long paddle was not a cakewalk but neither was it difficult.

Michelle's excitement grew to a crescendo as they came within two hundred feet of the landing. "Can you see the cabin, Annie?" she excitedly asked, already knowing the answer.

"No. Can you?"

"Yep, but that's only cause I know what to look for. If you don't know it's there, the place is invisible from the lake." One hundred feet away Michelle asked the same question, receiving the same answer. Annie never did spot the place. The Alumacraft rapidly approached the smooth granite landing. To Annie, it looked as though the canoe was going to slam into the shore. Michelle smiled as she saw Annie's back tense up.

"Don't worry; the canoe will glide effortlessly up on to shore. It's the perfect boat landing with no need for a dock." Annie relaxed when the canoe came to a smooth stop. She hopped out and pulled the canoe further onto shore, then straddled the craft so Michelle could safely exit. The timid woman silently absorbed the grandeur of the shore she now stood on. It was not like anything she had ever experienced before. The smooth granite, free of vegetation, gently sloped into the lake for about a hundred feet of the shoreline. It made for an interesting beach. There was no sand for bare feet to sink into. Annie loved walking on sandy beaches, letting the warm sand squish between her toes. Not having a sandy beach made her feel like she was visiting a different planet.

As much as she loved sand, she was not heartbroken that it was absent. The solid comfort of the rock gave Annie an overwhelming sense of security, like unto the wise man that built his house upon a rock. Annie stood on the landing and gazed off to the east not far from her. Her eyes followed the shoreline and shot up, tracing the contour of the granite bluff. She knew the view from on top would be incredible. For the little bit Annie just saw of the property, she was delighted. Michelle's description of the landing and beach area had not done the actual thing justice.

Michelle was sitting on a rock watching Annie's wandering eyes and was satisfied with her expression of awe. Michelle felt as though Annie just removed the bow from the present; she could not wait to give the rest of the tour.

"Can we go to the cabin now?" Annie asked with pleading eyes that were more green than brown at the moment.

"No," Michelle said with a patience she did not feel. "I want to wait till the others get here so everyone can see it at the same time." If Michelle gave Annie a tour of the property, she might miss out on showing it to the others. She knew DJ, having been here before, would take over the tour guide position. Michelle was not willing to share that honor with DJ today. Perhaps her attitude was selfish, but it was not without reason. Michelle worked long and hard building two log beds and doing other assorted projects for Carmen. A lot of her time and effort had been poured into securing this place for the weekend. She loved this place and had been in its little dream world the whole time she labored away on the beds. She knew the others would love it too. Michelle would not think of missing out on showing it to any of them. The anticipation of seeing the first impressions expressed on their faces kept her glued to the rock she sat on.

Michelle saw the Grumman off in the distance, but nearest in her mind was the thought, *If this is how I feel about sharing something that cost me so much, I wonder how much greater Christ's joy must be in sharing His gift of eternal life with others. I wish I could have seen His face and known His joy when first I accepted Him.*

The approaching canoe brought Michelle to her feet as her patient streak came to an abrupt end. She was pacing, barely able to tame the growing surge of anticipation. She grabbed the bow of the incoming Grumman, helping to further lodge it on shore. Annie was antsy as well and was very help-ful in lending a hand to unload the beached canoe. With everything unloaded onto the shore and the craft securely docked, Annie could no longer bear the suspense.

"We're all ready for the tour." Annie's pointed re-quest brought out a toothy smile from the leader.

"Well, let's not waste a trip; everybody grab a pack on your way up."

Annie grabbed her pack and followed Michelle up a natural progression of granite stairs that were cushioned by a fine carpet of dead needles. The reddish brown trail made its way up a little incline, meandering through the underbrush. The trail was not well defined. Annie could tell it was rarely used. Michelle paused to let the others catch up. She pointed to the ground.

"It's best to remember not to touch anything that's dead and down near the cabin. Carmen liked how these two branches fell." Annie studied the subject at hand.

"That looks like something my husband would bring home and mount on the wall."

"You're right, Annie. It looks like a trophy rack off a buck. Carmen's got a lot more of this type of stuff strategically placed—landscaping the cabin—mostly beaver driftwood. Sometimes she likes how something drops to the ground and she just leaves it there 'cause it looks natural. It's not her goal to have this place all manicured, looking like a public park, she wants it to look like the forest it is. So just leave everything the way you find it." Michelle turned and hiked on.

The trail ended before Annie realized it was over. There before her eyes was the phantom cabin. She now understood why she was not able to see it from the lake. It looked like a tree. Not the shape but the color. The logs were treated a silvery patina. The graining was clearly visible and beautiful; its weathered look blended magnificently with the neighboring tree trunks. The roof and trim were forest green in color. The large windows in each of the four walls allowed a penetrating glance straight through, camouflaging the fact that it was a solid structure. Annie wondered how many birds had been fooled like her into thinking there was nothing there. A quick walk around the cabin would have revealed the skeletons of many such unlucky birds.

Michelle unzipped her camera bag and found the key. She clutched the precious object and walked up the four half-log steps to the little log deck. She was nervous about the key. It was a duplicate that the hardware store recently cut for Carmen. The helpful hardware man assured Carmen that it was exactly the same as the original. Carmen gave it to Michelle saying, "I hope it works, I haven't tried it yet."

She inserted the key and turned it. Michelle breathed a sigh of relief when the door swung open. In her excitement, Michelle turned and smiled at the waiting ladies; she felt as though she should carry someone across the threshold. Annie was the closest and would be light. Michelle choked back a giggle and dismissed the thought as foolishness. She could not spontaneously embarrass anyone like that. There were times when she wished she had the courage to be more spontaneous. *It sure would make life more interesting,* she thought. Being dull and predictable was safer but definitely on the boring side. *I'll stick to boring,* she concluded.

The trapped cedar aroma escaped through the open door, serving as the official welcoming committee. As the ladies filed inside, Annie decided the cedar smell was simply delicious. Michelle's ears and eyes were alert as the ladies pored over every detail in the cabin. Karen marveled over the candle chandelier. Annie studied the woodstove and its cool heat shield, wondering how Carmen painted it to look like the woods on a foggy morning. DJ reacquainted herself with the cozy surroundings while Jenna checked out a log bed to see if it would hold her. Michelle's radar picked up the "oohs" and "ahhs" that echoed together, bouncing off the log walls. She was delighted to see the pleasurable expressions registering on the faces of the three newcomers. The ladies could not have been more thrilled.

Subduing her true emotions, Michelle calmly watched the ladies explore their new location. Michelle's hidden joy turned to hidden terror. She noticed something in the cabin the others missed and cringed at the sight of Jenna lying unawares on top of it. Karen tried out the other log bed; Michelle gasped and held her breath. When only she and DJ remained inside, the others leaving to haul up more gear, Michelle handed DJ a broom.

CHAPTER SEVENTEEN

COMIC RELIEF

There's mice in here, DJ! They've left their calling cards everywhere. Help me clean up the evidence before the ladies come back." They dusted windowsills, shook out bedspreads, wiped off the table, and swept the floor. The cumulative evidence made Michelle sick to her stomach. "I hate mice," she said with disgust. At that very moment, one of the despised rodents audaciously crawled up the wall in front of her very eyes. She was too slow with the broom to successfully swat it. Michelle was quietly calculating, *Five women, four beds, one mouse. Some one is going to get stuck on the floor and I hope it's not me.* She would have to tell the women about the mice. She did not feel right keeping that info from them. She knew there would be no brave volunteers for the floor.

Karen walked in with her pack and plopped it on the floor. "This place is way cool. I can't believe we're really staying here, ya know."

"I'll pinch you if ya need it," Michelle offered. Declining the offer, Karen sprawled out on one of the freshly de-moused beds. Michelle cringed, she wanted to tell Karen about the mice and the mess they made on that bedspread but did not have the heart seeing her lying there so comfortably. *Later,* she reasoned *I'll tell them all later.*

After all the gear was brought up to the cabin, Michelle finished the tour by showing the ladies where the latrine and the private swimming area were located. A more thorough exploration of the point would have to be done at a later time; everyone was hungry. Michelle was a degree beyond hungry; she was famished. She knew it would be a good while before supper could be started. Michelle needed to pump water for the meal and top off the drinking jugs. Pumping with a clogged filter would consume a lot of her time.

"Michelle?" DJ asked, "What's on the menu for supper?"

"Since you didn't catch us any fish, it's spaghetti." Michelle brought the spaghetti in case the fish were elusive, but otherwise, spaghetti was not her favorite meal. She did not look forward to consuming the stuff.

"Do you mind if I make supper tonight?" DJ asked cautiously, not wanting to seem pushy.

"That would be great. If you had to wait for me to make supper, it'd be at least another hour before I could get to it. I'm glad you asked."

"What else can I make to round out the meal?"

"Use whatever floats your boat. You'll have to look through the food pack and buckets to see what interests you." Michelle gathered the pump and jugs in her arms and left the determined and hungry chef to cook her masterpiece. Walking to the lake, she smiled as she thought of a little sign that hung on the wall above the stove in DJ's home. It said, "Never Trust a Skinny Cook." For some reason that thought momentarily amused Michelle.

As she walked, Michelle smiled and took a sentimental moment to reminisce on her friendship with DJ. Michelle treasured DJ's friendship as a woman would a diamond. She was precious to Michelle. It had taken several years for Michelle to come to that realization. DJ was not the type of person Michelle would have chosen for a friend. The slender lady was very talkative and friendly. Michelle preferred the challenge of befriending the quiet and shy. A shy person not only presented a challenge, but she would also allow her the opportunity to talk. It wasn't that Michelle would walk away with the person's ear—she was not by nature a talker—she just appreciated when someone listened with their full attention. She felt safe talking to shy people; they allotted her the time and space to safely express her thoughts in full.

Talkative people tended to mistake Michelle's pause as the end of her sentence. To be cut off in the middle of a thought or sentence was an agony worse than death for Michelle. She needed to fully express her thought and not have it cut off or interrupted mid-sentence. Michelle had a hard enough time expressing herself and could never regroup her train of thought once it was interrupted. Her thoughts, if completely voiced, often revealed an intimate relationship with her Savior. If she did not feel safe in a conversation, she would keep her unspoken thoughts under lock and key.

For years Michelle found it difficult to open up to DJ. In conversations, she kept waiting for DJ to take a breath and ask her a question or let her talk. Unbeknownst to Michelle, DJ wanted to ask her questions, but she felt as though she was prying where perhaps Michelle did not want her to. It was a vicious cycle that drove Michelle crazy. After years of this type of friendship, DJ made a comment about Michelle in front of her and Jerry. It started as an innocent conversation about husbands buying their wives presents with cords attached and how it was not a good idea. Jerry told of the successful woodworking present he had recently purchased and given to Michelle. He had given her a cordless drill. DJ's comment, "What would she do with that?" revealed that she did not think the gift was fitting for the recipient. The Paulsons looked at each other with eyes that relayed the silent message, "We need to talk later." That evening, in the privacy of their own home, they did talk.

"How long have you and DJ been friends?" Jerry asked his wife.

"A couple years. You're thinking about her comment, aren't you?"

"Yes, I am. She doesn't really know you, does she?"

"No, but that's probably my fault. I keep hoping she'll make inquires about my day, or week, or what I've been up to, or even what's been real to me from the Scriptures. The questions never come. I don't want to spill my guts out if she's not interested."

"You could volunteer the information."

"But—"

"No. Let me finish," Jerry said, interrupting as he read his wife's mind. "Just as I interrupted you, you can do that to her. If there's something you want to tell her, just tell her. She'll listen to you. You're not being fair to her by making her to do all the talking." Jerry was done; he said what was on his mind.

"I know; you're right. God will have to help me be more assertive." Michelle was serious and asked God for help and He delivered. She wanted to be a better friend to DJ. As she practiced being more assertive, looking for DJ's brief pauses, and interrupting when she felt it was OK, their friendship developed. It was now a couple years later. Michelle did not regret forcing herself to interrupt DJ. DJ was now as dear to her as Stephanie, her young adventurous buddy, and Joan, her older, more practical friend. Michelle's little world would be awful lonely without her talkative friend. DJ's midweek phone calls filled with comical stories brightened many long days for Michelle. Even Jerry looked forward to Michelle receiving a DJ call. She always relayed the funny stories to her husband, brightening up his week as well.

Thinking about DJ while pumping water helped Michelle endure the challenging task with a chuckle. Her comic relief did not change the fact that the pumping was slow and difficult. Michelle had to stop frequently to rest. After a bit, she filled up a pan with lake water and brought it to the cabin. She made Karen, Annie, and Jenna each take turns pumping. About the time the last jug was filled, DJ announced the meal call, much to the delight of the starving campers.

Spaghetti was an easy meal to make and also fairly cheap. Those two qualities were the reason Michelle's household consumed so many spaghetti dinners. The meal had long ago lost its luster in Michelle's mind. For her, spaghetti was something to be endured rather than enjoyed.

DJ expressed to God a heartfelt thank-you for the nourishment, and then each lady grabbed a plate and served up their portion in DJ's makeshift kitchen. DJ's choice cooking area was underneath the protective covering of the roof on the north gable end. A log bench served as a table, holding the cook stove and all the delectables. The ladies filled their plates from the buffet-style operation and walked inside to sit at the tree stump table. It was quite the spread, and Michelle was duly impressed. Somehow, DJ spiced up the spaghetti so that it was quite worthy of commendation. The skinny cook also did wonders to the bread, turning it into a seasoned garlic toast. The beef jerky on the side added the meat the meal was lacking. Michelle consumed her spaghetti in short order and went out for seconds.

As Michelle situated herself at the table once again, a sinister thought entered her head. The thought had actually been there for many years, it was now just coming back to her memory. To do what she was thinking would almost be spontaneous. Spontaneous meant dangerous—not safe. If she tried and pulled this off, someone would be embarrassed. This prank would be aimed right at DJ.

The spaghetti triggered a memory of a couple wacky roommates to whom Michelle once rented to before being married. The renters were two of the zaniest ladies Michelle had ever met. They were both named Annie. Little redheaded Annie had prepared a spaghetti supper in honor of Big Annie's first date. Big Annie's date, Sam, sat shyly next to her, while Michelle and Little Annie, occupied the other two seats. While Little Annie engaged her roommate's date in conversation, Big Annie slyly pulled out some of her hair and slipped it onto her plate, mixing it into her spaghetti.

Michelle, sitting to Big Annie's left at the round table, was dumbfounded and pretended not to see the odd behavior. The others missed it completely.

Michelle kept her eyes open to see what would happen next. Big Annie took a forkful of the mixture and put it in her mouth. Next thing Michelle knew, Big Annie was gagging and pulling the hair out of her mouth, making a big spectacle of the foreign objects. As she pulled one hair after the other out of her food, the other two could be seen examining their plates more closely. Michelle had to excuse herself to go to the bathroom before she exploded with laughter. Little Annie, being the chef, felt awful about the hair and was puzzled as to how it came to be in her creation. Big Annie's date left that night and never came back.

Big Annie later confessed she pulled the stunt to get rid of her stuffy date. The humor in the prank had not been lost on Michelle, and now she sat toying with the idea of trying it herself. The other ladies contentedly feasted on the meal and were full of praise for the chef. Hearing the gratitude from the others, Michelle repented, and set aside her sinister plan, deciding not to ruin the perfect meal for DJ. Hiding a smile, Michelle sighed; once again she chose the safe and boring route of being considerate. Just once she'd like to be spontaneous.

Michelle topped off her meal with grape Kool-Aid and tapioca pudding. Her hunger pains vanished, and she sat wondering if she could roll off her chair and out the door to start the cleanup. Karen interrupted her thought to volunteer herself and Jenna for the dishes duty.

The rest of the evening was spent cleaning up, exploring, swimming, and just lounging around. There was nothing planned until the evening devotion. Jenna sprawled out on one of the log beds, lying on her back with her hands under her head. She closed her eyes, shutting out the rest of the room. The world under her eyelids was private and very contemplative. Once again she mulled over her thoughts for the devotion. Jenna did not plan out devotions the way she planned events. She felt it unnecessary to have every word mapped out; she put a topic in her mind and added living and breathing truths from the Bible and then let God process the data. When the devotion left her lips, it was an expression of an impromptu heart-to-heart, not a polished political speech.

The devotion she purposed to give tonight was a lesson she recently learned from the patient hand of her loving Savior. She marveled at how patient her God really was with her. Sometimes she felt like a dunce for taking so long to learn a lesson. Jenna had trained herself to have a critical eye, to always look at situations and circumstances, and to peel away layers until a spiritual lesson could be gleaned. Her attitude was always one of "What can I learn from this situation?" She looked at the Scriptures that way as well, seeking divine lessons from each reading and looking for ways the truth might be expounded upon in her daily life. When daily life and spiritual lessons collided, a new truth would be mastered.

Jenna eagerly shared her lessons with others, hoping that the hearer would avoid the mistakes she made and benefit from the virtual lesson. Her recitations of personal experiences and mastered truths gave one a little glimpse of her love affair with her great God and Savior. "Oh Lord," she silently prayed, "please help me tonight to share what's on my heart and to make my utterances as clear to the group as You first made it to me."

The ladies were stirring in the cabin, trying to figure out where to set up their sleeping bags. Michelle sat by the table, patiently waiting to see the outcome; she had leaked the mouse news earlier. *Five women, four beds, one mouse. Who will get the floor?*

The trundle beds were pulled out and set up next to the log beds. Jenna was already lying on a log bed and Karen was making herself comfortable on the trundle next to Jenna. On the opposite side of the room, Annie and DJ were politely discussing who should get which bed. Annie claimed the other log bed and DJ settled into the trundle. "Annie," Michelle said reservedly, "I wouldn't put your sleeping bag that way with your head next to the wall if I were you."

"Why?" Annie asked, puzzled.

"That's where I saw the mouse crawl up the wall, and it's also the location on the bed where the largest pile of mouse droppings were."

"Oh. Thanks, I'll switch the bag around."

Annie and DJ had their beds all situated before they realized that Michelle was doomed to the floor.

Annie spoke first. "Michelle, I am so sorry, I didn't even ask you if you wanted a bed to sleep on. Would you like this bed? I can take the floor."

"Or you could have my bed," DJ added.

Karen and Jenna were offering theirs too. Michelle was feeling awkward with all the attention focused on her. She would not dream of putting Karen, the eldest, on the floor, or Jenna, with her bad back. Michelle felt DJ needed a good night's sleep and should have a bed. And as for Annie, she wanted her to be comfortable, too. She would not feel right asking Annie to give up her bed. Michelle resigned herself to sleep on the floor.

"I'll be OK on the floor. With two air mattresses under me, I'll be as comfortable as if I were on a bed." And the truth was that she would be. Michelle would just have to trust the Lord to protect her from the mouse. That was her only reservation about the floor. *Maybe tonight I'll sleep with the broom next to me instead of the hatchet,* she thought to herself.

The ladies were thoroughly tired after the hot, draining day. No one wanted to fight the sandman tonight. Preparations were made for bed with DJ's chatter filling the room like background music. Everyone was sitting on her bed, ready and waiting for Jenna's devotion. DJ realized her mouth was the only one moving as the ladies politely listened to the conclusion of her story. Jenna loudly cleared her throat to capture the entire audience. DJ's mouth opened, but before a sound could escape, she shut it, took her fingers to her lips, and zipped an imaginary zipper. A pretend key secured the lock to her mouth and was placed in her pocket.

Devotion time was a silent torture for DJ. She had to consciously remind herself to be quiet to listen, and not to interrupt. To DJ, it was a feeling similar to that of taking a deep breath and holding it while swimming under water; eventually she would burst and have to surface for air. She comforted herself by acknowledging the fact that she could burst in about fifteen minutes. She could handle this trial. Having everyone's attention, Jenna prayed and proceeded to share her learned lesson.

"I've been reading through Job lately but not finding a whole lot of content relevant to my life. I had to stop and ask God to make something stand out for me so that I could walk away with something personal. That's when I came to Job chapter six, and I'll read verses four to eight, showing how Job at first had a bad attitude. He thought he had a right to complain.

"'For the arrows of the Almighty are within me; my spirit drinks in their poison; the terrors of God are arrayed against me. Does the wild donkey bray when it has grass, or does the ox low over its fodder? Can flavorless food be eaten without salt? Or is there any taste in the white of an egg? My soul refuses to touch them; they are as loathsome food to me. Oh, that I might have my request, that God would grant me the thing that I long for.'

"After I read and reread that portion, it struck me how much I was like Job. Sometimes I feel that

I have the right to complain about tasteless food, the weather, slow traffic, vehicle breakdowns, my husband's shortcomings, or anything else. Whether the complaining is verbally spoken or mentally thought, I often feel justified in my mumbling and grumbling. This portion of Scripture presented a question for me to ponder. If it wasn't right for Job to complain, is it ever right and just for me to complain? God took me to Philippians 2:14–16 and answered the question for me.

"'Do all things without grumbling and disputing, that you may become blameless and harmless, children of God without fault in the midst of a crooked and perverse generation, among whom you shine as lights in the world, holding fast the word of life, so that I may rejoice in the day of Christ that I have not run in vain or labored in vain.'"

The devotion struck a nerve with DJ, causing her to tune out Jenna's voice. She was mentally examining all the times she had felt justified in complaining. DJ's spirit left the confines of the little log cabin and entered the throne room of her heavenly Father. A silent heartfelt prayer for forgiveness and divine help arose like the smoke of celestial incense. Before DJ knew it, Jenna wrapped up her devotion, leaving everyone with something to think about, and prayed. Last-minute preparations for bed were made, pillows were fluffed, sleeping bags adjusted, and "Good nights" were exchanged.

When everyone was settled, Michelle found her headlamp, blew out the candles, and crawled into her sleeping bag. Even though she was on the floor at the mercy of a little rodent, she felt safe. Her head rested peacefully on the pillow, her left hand held the headlamp ready at a moment's notice, and her right hand was open and free. It was ready to reach for the broom should she hear the scampering of little feet. Michelle was exhausted but happy. She had a lot to thank God for and did so silently. She was about to enter slumber land when Jenna's whispered voice startled her.

"Michelle, I hear voices. It sounds like someone's outside our window."

Wondering where she put the hatchet, Michelle stood up and shone her light around the room, looking for the sharp object. She heard the voices too and looked out the window. Michelle saw the light of a boat passing by and breathed a bit easier. The sound of the passengers was magnified by the still night and open water. "It's just a boat passing by," Michelle reassuringly informed Jenna. To put her own mind more at ease, she locked the door before slipping back into her bag.

This time Michelle had fallen into a deep sleep before being awakened by DJ's ear-piercing scream. "*Michelle!*"

Michelle jumped up with haste, turning on her flashlight, not knowing if she should grab the broom or the hatchet. "What's wrong, DJ?"

The slender woman was in hysterics. "The mouse! The mouse! It was on top of me, running across my bag!"

Michelle wanted to laugh in relief but decided to remain serious in her friend's great moment of need. In an attempt to calm DJ, Michelle flashed her light back and forth across the cabin, searching for the mouse that elicited such a death-defying scream. With no sign of the rodent, Michelle gave up in defeat, thanking God that she wasn't the one the mouse decided to crawl into bed with. *The mouse probably found a quiet little spot to have a coronary,* Michelle thought as she drifted back to sleep.

Karen woke up in the middle of the night and felt disoriented. The clouds had blown in and robbed all natural light from view. She tried to open her eyes as wide as possible to see her surroundings but realized she was totally blind. Even though her eyes were open, she could not see anything but blackness. She put her hand in front of her face with it touching her nose but was unable to see even that. Never before had she experienced total darkness. It was a creepy, cool experience for the woman. She started to wonder if this was a normal darkness or if the half a painkiller she chewed up before going to bed was playing tricks on her mind. Whatever the darkness was caused from, she was so thankful it was blackness she was seeing rather than pink elephants. Karen needed to take a little hike outside but thought better of waking Jenna. Her hike would wait till morning.

CHAPTER EIGHTEEN

HEART AND SOUL

The rest of the night was passed in peaceful slumber. Michelle, refreshed by the good night's sleep, woke with the rising sun. She took advantage of the quiet cabin, reading Scripture to prepare her mind for the busy day ahead. Knowing that she would have to leave this place today, a little cloud of sadness hung over her heart. The thought of coming back over Labor Day weekend was the ray of sunshine that chased away the darkness. She would not allow herself to dwell on the sorrow of parting, not today. When the others began to stir, Michelle slipped outside to begin breakfast.

DJ put her shoes on and excused herself from the cabin to make the little hike to the latrine. When Michelle saw her pass by, she chuckled, remembering the night before. The little mouse was nothing compared to the bear DJ encountered last Labor Day weekend. On that trip, DJ had gone alone to the latrine one night and was startled by a rustling in the woods next to her seat. She quickly finished her business and slammed the latrine cover as hard as she could, hoping to scare off the intruder. She took off running toward the cabin while the large animal took off in the direction of Michelle and Jerry's tent. Michelle heard the slam and knew where DJ had just been. Moments later, she too heard something rather large pass by her tent. The next morning a good-sized fish lay dead in the middle of the trail close to the latrine. DJ more than likely scared that poor animal to death causing it to leave its fish supper behind. DJ was practiced at scaring helpless animals.

Michelle's syrup-less pancakes were done and set on the table. The ladies were cautious, not knowing what to think of the odd breakfast.

"What's in it?" DJ asked genuinely interested.

"Chocolate chips, also peanut butter, butterscotch, and mint chips too. See, that way I didn't need to bring syrup, they're already sweet and gooey enough." The pancakes were not a big hit. Michelle liked them and so did her family. She could not understand why the ladies hardly touched the meal. She was not too worried about them starving. She knew they would feel at liberty to invade the snack containers if hungry later. Michelle wondered why she had bothered to bring any real food with her. The ladies barely touched any of the meals she had prepared. The only meal that had been a hit was DJ's spaghetti supper. Michelle was wondering if her cooking was really that bad. *That's probably why my husband's so skinny*, she concluded.

It made Michelle sick to her stomach to have to throw away so much food, but the table needed to be cleared and breakfast stuff put away. The plateful of pancakes went in the garbage. When everything was tidied up, the ladies sat patiently, each on their own bed. Annie was getting her notes and Bible together to give the morning devotion.

Annie was not chewing on her fingernails, but inwardly she felt like she was. The whole trip had been a nail-biting experience for her. She was unsure of herself each step of the way, not knowing if she could physically or mentally tackle each new twist and turn of the trip. A bit of her old fear always loomed in the background threatening to swallow her up and shut her down if the pressure grew unbearable. During the trip, her appearance remained calm due in part to a false confidence and security she derived from the leader of the group. She was to an extent trusting in Michelle's misleadingly calm leadership. If she would have had any insight at all into the fears that Michelle wrestled with, Annie would have crumbled. Fear was a formidable foe to this timid woman.

Annie began her devotion after a short prayer. Each woman in the room listened with rapt attention, looking for insights into Annie's heart and soul. "When Michelle asked me to prepare a devotion for this trip, I really struggled with what to share. I knew I couldn't talk about something that wasn't real to me, so I decided to talk about fear."

At the mention of fear, Michelle hung on every word Annie spoke.

"I am the type of person who is easily frightened. Fear has a way of swallowing me up. Not too long ago, I battled with this fear monster. I couldn't go anywhere or do anything without this hideous beast rearing its ugly head and putting doubts in my mind. If I went for a drive, I would start to worry that I would get into a crash and kill my kids. If I went to the grocery store, I feared that I would have a panic attack and leave all my groceries behind. I struggled with going anywhere in public afraid I'd have a heart attack and never make it home.

"The fears were unfounded, I wasn't in any real danger, but I did it to myself. I embraced the monster, and it grew. I gave fear a place in my heart and it shut me down. For a long time I didn't drive; I refused to go anywhere. I never went out in public, and I quit conversing with my family. No one knew what was going on inside of me, not even my husband. No one could help me. I lived in a constant state of terror. It felt as though I was on an airplane, knowing it was going to crash. I would break out in sweat, and my heart pounded as though it was looking for a way to escape my chest. It was sheer terror. I wanted help; I knew I couldn't go on living like that anymore. I had created my own personal nightmare.

"In my own way of reaching out for help, I ordered an 'Attacking Panic' tape set from a TV infomercial. The set was expensive, but it was really helpful. The principles in it were excellent, but I still lacked the power to change. It wasn't until I opened my Bible that I experienced where the real life-changing power came from. I looked up verses on fear such as Philippians 4:6–7.

"'Be anxious for nothing, but in everything by prayer and supplication, with thanksgiving, let your requests be made known to God; and the peace of God, which surpasses all understanding, will guard your hearts and minds through Christ Jesus.'

"The more I dwelt on and meditated on the Scriptures, the less I thought about myself. I was learning to, as 1 Peter 5:7 says, 'cast all your cares upon Him, for he cares for you.' Second Timothy 1:7 reminded me, when I would forget, that 'God has not given us the spirit of fear, but of power and of love and of a sound mind.' As I sought the Lord for help, Psalm 34:4 proved true: 'He heard me and delivered me from all my fears.' Through the power of God's Word, He gave me the victory over my enemy: anxiety. To this day, when I start to feel the paralyzing fear reaching for my mind, I have to grab a verse and ruminate on it much the same way a cow chews on its cud. I have to jump with my whole heart into a verse, dissect it word by word, and meditate on the meaning of each syllable. I have to surround myself with Scripture and apply it to my situation. This all takes work and effort, but to taste God's victory and to be able to say as Paul did, 'I can do all things through Christ which strengthens me,' that is real joy and real peace. God has helped me to lessen the number of anxiety attacks, and I trust some day He will completely remove them. And that is how God has been working in my life."

The ladies thanked Annie for her devotion and after a bit of discussion the cabin emptied, leaving Annie and Michelle sitting on a log bed.

"Annie," Michelle said, avoiding eye contact as she looked out the picture window nearest her, "I wish you would have given your devotion the first night." Michelle did not give Annie a chance to ask why. "I think I might have slept better thinking about your devotion and its practical application rather than the fears that robbed me of sleep." Michelle turned to see Annie's puzzled expression but offered no more explanation. Annie did not press her; she wasn't sure she really wanted to know or could even handle the knowledge of the fear Michelle alluded to. Annie eventually concluded that perhaps Michelle was teasing her, for she was often hard to read. At times Michelle teased using the same straight face she would use to relay serious life and death information.

Annie quit trying to figure her out, while Michelle marveled at her changing eye colors. Michelle studied Annie and decided her irises looked more brown today than green. Annie's dark curly hair was neatly tucked back in a ponytail and her tanned arms, with her white tank top for a backdrop, looked so brown crossed in front of her. The green in her eyes lay dormant, letting the showier brown match her tan and hair. Deciding that Annie's Italian heritage was making itself known today, Michelle tore her gaze from the chameleon eyes.

Michelle was enjoying getting to know this unique lady and was momentarily saddened that they would only have a few more hours together before the trip was over. Sensing that Annie's barrier, her wall of self-preservation, was starting to crumble, Michelle decided to patiently keep chiseling. She wanted Annie's friendship and had waited almost ten years for Annie to catch on. Michelle could not bear the thought of waiting another ten years. She had always felt that Annie would make for a good friend; she never wavered in that conviction. A scary thought entered Michelle's mind. She could picture herself and Annie being old and gray, confined to wheelchairs, sitting in a nursing home, with Michelle finally finding the courage to ask Annie, "Will you be my friend?" Michelle shuddered at the thought of such wasted time.

Retrieving her mind from the future, Michelle asked Annie a question that was purposely designed to take another carving blow at the barrier. "What were you like as a young child? Were you controlled by fear then too?"

Startled by the question, Annie pondered her reply. To answer this question truthfully would be unsafe. She weighed the odds and decided to be truthful rather than to hide behind the comfort of her shyness. "In elementary school," Annie paused to take a deep breath, "I was extremely quiet. I was afraid to make eye contact with anyone, and I definitely didn't talk any more than I had to. Because I was so quiet, kids picked on me everywhere I went. I felt powerless to defend myself so I just sat there and took it, never saying a word in protest. My school bus rides were the worst. A tall skinny girl named Erica turned them into a living nightmare. The girl once took my schoolbooks and dangled them out the window. When I didn't say a word, she threw them on the ground. The bus driver was more upset with me that he had to stop the bus so I could retrieve my books. I'll never forget picking up my poor books and seeing the huge tire tracks on them.

"That wasn't the only incident with Erica. Day after day she would hover over me and pick my barrettes out of my hair one by one and toss them out the bus window. One time she even took my home economic assignment and threw that out the window, too. That was a terrible day for me. I had so carefully guarded and protected my "baby" from harm. My "baby" was an egg the teacher had assigned to me—everyone in the class had one—to take care of. We had to treat that egg like a real baby, finding babysitters for it and everything. I never left it alone, and I even made clothes for it. I was so proud of my "baby," so you can imagine how choked up I got when Erica killed my "baby."

"I must have looked pathetic sitting on that bus cowering from Erica like a frightened little bug about to be squashed. One of the bigger boys came to my rescue; he took me to sit by him in the back. He said he got fed up with how I was being treated and that I'd be safe by him. I was so thankful for that boy. I can't begin to describe the fear I felt. I lived with a constant terror bottled up inside me every day of my young life. As a teenager that compressed fear turned to anger and it found ways to spill out."

Annie stopped and, for the time being, Michelle dared not to ask any more pointed questions. Trying to comprehend Annie as an angry teenager, Michelle stood up to think and walked to the window. She leaned against the trim, looked out at the bright blue sky, and decided to change the subject. "It's a beauty out. Wanna go for a swim?"

CHAPTER NINETEEN

WHITECAPS

Relieved to be done talking, Annie gave a consenting smile. The two ladies suited up, grabbed their towels, and left the cabin. Outside by the clothesline, Annie and Michelle found the other three women standing around putting sunscreen on each other's backs. They were suited up as well and ready for a swim. Michelle, not wanting to later wear a wet life jacket, was the only who did not bring one to the swimming area. The others, less sure of their swimming abilities, quickly snapped on their life jackets and followed Michelle to the lake.

It was extremely windy out, with tree branches snapping everywhere and falling to the ground. Michelle knew how dangerous it was to walk through the woods on a day like this. She kept a careful watch upward as she went. Michelle was relieved that this wind was not accompanied by a creepy green sky. To be out in the woods during a tornado was no picnic.

As a teenager, she had been camping in the BWCA when a tornado hit. It came in the middle of the night with a wind so ferocious that Michelle and her companion had to put their legs up in the air to keep the tent from caving in. Rivers of water rushed in and through the tent. The two friends stacked all their clothes and sleeping bags into a heap to try to keep some of it dry. Their efforts were not fruitful. At daybreak, the exhausted, wet women emerged from the tent to see the destruction that surrounded them. Trees were down everywhere, with one lying only two feet away from the other tent. They felt blessed to be alive, and only after they left the BWCA did they find out for sure that it had been a tornado. Michelle had no desire to relive that experience.

Before getting to the lake, she already knew what to expect. Her suspicion was confirmed with one look at the rough water. Michelle studied the whitecaps and whispered a silent thank you to God. As long as the wind kept blowing in the direction it was, Michelle would not allow herself to worry. The wind would later be pushing them to their exit point rather than fighting them. If the wind shifted, Michelle feared the ladies would cry out like the faithless disciples once did: "Lord, don't you care we are about to die?" For now Michelle shoved aside her worst fear and decided to embrace the wind and enjoy it. Whitecaps could be fun, and she wanted the ladies to immerse themselves in this experience. With a running leap she jumped into the foamy lake. If the ladies followed her example, they would gain a healthy respect for the power of this white water.

The waves rushed Michelle down the shoreline where she eventually crawled out back onto dry land. The little ride was enjoyable, and she went to repeat it again. The others followed, and they too found pleasure in the swim. DJ was growing accustomed to the security of her life jacket and looked like a little kid happily splashing around in the water. Jenna left her serious side on shore, and mindful of her back, she carefully let herself into the water. She also found the sport of the ride enjoyable. Karen wanted to reserve her strength for the rough canoe ride home, so she spent only a short time in the lake. The trip had taken its toll on Karen; a good part of yesterday found her drained and ill, lying on her bed. She was doing better today but knew her limits would be tested. Annie was warier of the whitecaps. It took a lot of convincing on Michelle's part to get her wet. She only indulged in the ride a couple times before she lay down to sun herself on the security of the warm rock.

Sitting on the granite boulder, Karen watched the three "kids" play in the water. She smiled at the sight of their antics. She felt blessed to be on the trip spending time with her daughter and getting to know these ladies. The comfort of the warm rock, the fact that she was not starving, the wind blowing in her hair, and having time to herself away from work all contributed to the overwhelming feeling of peace that swallowed her up. She felt as though she was sitting in a little Eden without a care in the world. It would not be easy for her to leave this place. Karen's hectic lifestyle kept her on the run with no time for contemplation. As she sat in her state of peace, she purposed to slow down. She resolved to make time for the hearing of God's Word and for more camping. She was making a mental list of all the gear she would need to buy to be able to do this on her own. She was already planning her next trip. Karen wondered if she could get her mother to go with her.

Michelle climbed out of the water to do the ride again and decided to do something spontaneous. She shook out her hair like a wet dog on the back of the sunning Annie Ojala. Michelle ran away and jumped into the water before Annie could rebuke her. Annie chuckled to herself and shot a smile at Michelle who was bobbing by in the water. Michelle winked back. Jenna, swimming next to Michelle, was concerned for their leader. She could tell Michelle was working too hard without her life jacket to stay afloat. They couldn't afford to have Michelle drown. She swam to shore and disappeared. Moments later Jenna was back and threw Michelle's life jacket out to her.

"Thanks." Michelle said as she worked to get into the preserver. "You must have been reading my mind."

"My motive was purely selfish, Michelle, we don't know how to get back to the boat landing without you." Jenna's teasing tone camouflaged her real motive, which was not at all selfish. She had seen their leader work very hard to ensure the comfort of the ladies, taking more chores upon herself so the others could relax. Jenna kept her eyes open for opportunities to show Michelle her appreciation through little gestures of kindness. She wanted Michelle to enjoy the trip as much as she was.

Jenna swam out to DJ and Michelle and found herself doing synchronized swimming moves with DJ. Giving the two friends some space to play, Michelle swam a little further away. She was happy to see the friends reconnect and had known that Jenna's busy schedule with the credit union, church, and her husband had left DJ lonesome for Jenna. When Jenna moved to the Iron Range, DJ wasted no time in befriending her. The ladies had spent countless hours together shopping, visiting, and being spontaneous. The quick-witted and fun-loving Jenna proved to be a good listener for the talkative DJ. Whenever DJ encountered strange dilemmas with tricky problems, Jenna lent a listening ear and also sought to find reasonable solutions or suggestions for the situation. Jenna loved a good challenge and was the type of person who could easily spend days thinking about someone else's problem. She enjoyed figuring out solutions to help people out.

From a distance, Michelle admired Jenna's ability to make DJ laugh. She was funny without even trying. Michelle was getting the impression that Jenna would be the type of person to make any ordinary event fun. *I'll bet she's a sight to see at home in her kitchen*, Michelle thought. *She'd likely be the one to wear Saran Wrap around her head to protect her eyes from onion gasses. She'd be totally oblivious to the fact of how humorously odd she'd look to those around her.*

Jenna's theatrical expressions and reactions to good news and bad news alike earned her the title of the "Drama Queen." Her coworkers at the credit union affectionately gave her the moniker. As much as Michelle admired Jenna's wit, she had long ago come to the realization that she herself lacked that quality.

In high school, Michelle adored the drama students. She loved how they made people laugh on stage and off. She tried in vain to fit into their group and had thought she was making progress, when Rita, a drama queen in her own right, asked her to hang out. Rita took the ecstatic Michelle to go visit their actor friend, Chad. Michelle didn't care where she went just as long as she could be around Rita.

Michelle made a total fool out of herself trying to keep up with the witty humor of the other two. Following that initial outing with Rita, it was Chad who hung out with Michelle after that. Michelle would have preferred hanging out with Rita, but Chad was fun to be around, too. She enjoyed Chad's friendship but thought he worked too hard to be different. He was not normal. He never wore clothes that looked good or stylish. He preferred florescent orange polyester pants to regular blue jeans, and he always made sure his shirts and socks were of equally bold colors to clash with his pants. It was a sin for him to actually look stylish. His fashion statement was probably why he lacked a serious girlfriend. Michelle had found it weird that Rita had so easily befriended her but then left her to hang out with Chad.

The light bulb in Michelle's head finally went on, illuminating Rita's odd behavior. After a football game one Friday night, Chad took Michelle out for pizza. When they left the restaurant, Chad shocked Michelle by reaching for her hand. In a daze, she pulled it away. He reached for it again and asked what was wrong. Michelle sorted out the implications of Chad's action and realized that Rita had set her up. She felt like a fool. Not sure how to best inform Chad that she had no intention of dating him and becoming the laughing stock of the school, she said the first thing that came to her mind. "I can't date you because I don't know who I am." Michelle's odd response threw Chad for a loop, and they remained just friends.

After that incident, Michelle abandoned her dream of being a thespian and dumped all thoughts of trying out for the high school play. She decided to stick to her less spontaneous and uncreative sports of track and cross-country running. To satisfy her creative side, she poured her heart and soul into safer solo activities such as woodworking, drawing, and painting. Trying to fit into a group of comedians had been too draining for Michelle. She decided it was definitely not her calling in life. She would, however, continue to admire the theatrically-inclined.

Michelle floated closer to the two friends and observed them play. With a twinkle in her eye, Jenna studied the calm DJ. She was glad to see her friend enjoying the water. She remembered swimming with a frantic DJ a couple years earlier. Using borrowed lifejackets that were way too small, the two friends had let the current of the St. Louis River take them on a route that could be repeated over and over. They played together in the river supported only by their lifejackets and a couple of fun "noodle" floaties. DJ did not feel secure in the undersized lifejacket and had displayed an acutely animated case of hydro-phobia. The frantic woman eventually calmed down when a larger-sized preserver was borrowed. Once she felt safe, DJ proceeded to teach Jenna a song about a freckled-faced crawdad that floated down the Misterslippi sipping on a jug of sassafras tea. That day had been enjoyable.

The ladies were in no hurry to leave the water, but growling stomachs told them it was time to start drying off. Spreading out on top of her Snoopy beach towel, Michelle laid on her belly with her head cush-ioned by her arms. She was a few feet from Annie, and well aware that Annie's beautiful tanned skin clashed loudly with her own rough farmer's tan. Silently chuckling inside about her observation, she mused over the fact that she didn't really care. Not too long ago, obtaining an even tan would have been a consuming goal early in the spring. But here it was already the middle of July and this trip was the first time her upper shoulders had seen the sun.

Being in a state of relaxation, Michelle almost drifted off to sleep. Hearing some motion, she lifted up her head to see Karen still sitting on the rock looking off into the wind with her dry hair floating on the strong breeze. Seeing Jenna to her left, Michelle asked, "How did your mom's hair dry so fast?"

"She combed it with her pick. Do you want to use her pick, too?"

"Oh, I wouldn't feel right asking to use her pick," Michelle said as she laid her head back onto her arms.

Jenna didn't say anything but quietly stood up and went to borrow her mother's pick. She sat down and picked through Michelle's long brown hair till it was free of tangles. Jenna's simple act of sweetness sent Michelle's mind whirling back to her high school days when all the girls would fuss over each other's hair. The little gesture of kindness was not wasted on Michelle. "Thank you, Jenna, that was real sweet of you."

"You're welcome."

Michelle sat up and let the wind take her hair. Since being out here, she noticed the velocity of the wind increase. The whitecaps were huge and showed no sign of letting up. Clouds were also blowing in. A good storm was probably not too far off. A new urgency surged through Michelle. "Ladies, I think we need to get back to the cabin, eat lunch, and think about packing up. There's more than likely a storm blowing in on this wind, and I don't want to get caught in the middle of it."

Michelle was torn. A part of her was frantic, wanting to make haste, pack, and leave; the other part calm and rational. She decided not to give into fear. She was not going to panic. Michelle was going to let herself enjoy what was left of the trip without rushing it to end. She took the ladies the long way back to the cabin so they could explore the other shoreline and see the view from the bluffs.

On one of the bluffs, the women, all having their cameras, wanted to stop and pose next to a very unique tree. The short, deformed white pine was pathetically beautiful. In the days of its youth, the tree had probably provided a tasty meal for a deer. The tip was missing and retarded further growth of the tree. Only one gnarled limb reached out from the eight-foot tall trunk. The roots were clearly visible, having less than an inch of acidic pine needle soil to hide in. The unfeeling granite bluff was a cruel place for the dwarf tree to exist. The tree expressed a sense of hope in the midst of despair.

"This is Carmen's 'Buddy Tree,'" Michelle stated, after all the pictures were done. "Before she owned this property, she would canoe to this spot, climb up the hill, and sit under this very tree. Each time she came she would bring dirt to put on top of its roots. She enjoyed the view of the lake from here and felt comfortable meditating on things. Carmen made a silent pact with the tree. In exchange for the pleasure of sitting in its shadow, she would take care of it the best she could."

Taking one last look at the little tree, the group pushed on, making their way back to the cabin. They prepared lunch and ate. When the meal was finished, the ladies still sitting at the table were careful to give their full attention to DJ. Her devotion was the last one to be given. DJ cleared her throat, prayed, and proceeded to share her thoughts.

"Several years ago I was visiting with a mutual friend of Michelle's and mine. In confidentiality this person told me 'I like Michelle as a friend, but I don't think she needs to bring the Lord into every conversation. There are other things to talk about in life.' At the time I agreed with this person and felt it would be extremely boring to include the Lord in every conversation. Since then I have changed my mind. Recently, in reading through Micah, I was overwhelmed with what an awesome God we have. I could not quit thinking about His greatness and splendor. This great God of ours has not only given us the very air we breathe and food we eat and every provision needed for existence, but as Micah asks, 'Who is a God like you, who pardons our sins, casting them into the depths of the sea and who delights in mercy?' Christ forgiving our sins is a powerful thing, but His power does not stop there.

"He is the Lord of the whole earth who will some day set foot once again on this planet. His feet will touch the mountain of God and it will melt under Him, and the valleys will split like wax before the fire. He will reign from Mount Zion over all the earth. He will bring something to the earth that no one before has ever brought—everlasting peace. There will be no need for military training; people will beat their swords into plowshares and their spears into pruning hooks. All war will cease. The nations will no longer rise against each other. The Lord will drive away the very fear of war. In that day many nations shall flow to the house of the Lord on their own free accord to be taught the ways of the Lord, to learn how to walk in His paths. They will go to worship and adore the Lord God.

"And what does this awesome and powerful God require of us as His children? Micah tells us it is simply to do justly, to love mercy, and to walk humbly with our God. If we are walking humbly with our God, whom will we be bragging about? It will not be about our measly accomplishments, but instead we will be boasting about our great God who accomplished something despite ourselves. We will want to tell everyone how God showed Himself real, powerful, and intimate. We will be so focused on giving Him the glory and credit He deserves. When we are filled with the awe of God, it will be so natural to spill His praises and include Him in our thoughts and words. Listening to a Christian talk about himself is boring. It is much more thrilling to hear a saint lovingly share about the Lord's accomplishments.

"The fact remains that there are so many things to talk about, but why not include the Lord in the conversation and make Him feel welcome rather than to exclude Him and ignore the Giver of all such pleasantries? For truly, all good gifts are from the Lord. He deserves a proper thank you. I know I very much like to hear people tell me 'thank you' and give me credit for something well done. How much more does our Lord desire due credit to be channeled to Him? To walk in the name of the Lord our God does not mean we give Him lip service on Sundays only, but the rest of the week our lips are moving for Him as well. And with that thought I will conclude this devotion."

Some of the ladies commented about the devotion and thanked DJ for her encouraging words. Michelle sat silently studying the wooden plugs on the edge of the table that hid the screw holes. She was pale and feeling sick to her stomach. Her sick feeling was not due to anything she ate but rather what DJ had said about her. It didn't bother her that someone had not enjoyed visiting with her in the past, she didn't even care to know who that was DJ spoke of. What was eating at her was the fact that it was now easier for her to talk about her kids rather than the Lord. Usually, the first thing to come out of her mouth was stories of her kids. People always seemed to begin a conversation with Michelle on the topic of her children, or current projects, or business. It had grown difficult for Michelle to transition the topics to include the Lord. She found herself speaking less and less about the Lord and more about herself, the kids, and the husband.

"Oh Lord, if I keep my mouth shut for You, the rocks will cry out. Please help me not to steal the glory and credit You deserve for Your accomplishments in my life." When the silent prayer was finished, the color in Michelle's face returned. At the sound of a rather large tree branch hitting the ground close to the cabin, Michelle's attention shifted to the growing whitecaps and the impending storm. The urgency was back and she knew it was not to be ignored. Interrupting the chattering women, Michelle announced, "We need to pack up quickly. Don't bother washing the dishes; I'll clean them when I get home." The room was a blur of activity as everyone pitched in and helped pack up.

DJ straightened up the cabin, now void of personal belongings. Together both she and Michelle washed the floor. DJ tiptoed back in over the wet floor and put the rugs in place. Michelle locked the door behind DJ and double-checked to see it was secure. She held on to the doorknob a moment longer, trying to convey a heartfelt farewell to the place of her daydreams. "See you in September," she said at last, forcing herself to turn away and head for the canoes.

CHAPTER TWENTY

PARALYZING FEAR

Looking over the packs, Michelle instructed the women to tie everything into the canoes. Bungies and ropes securely spider-webbed the gear into the canoes. Michelle took one last glance of the beach area and spotted the "Container of Death." She jogged over and picked up the white Styrofoam container. With Michelle's nose scrunched up, the contents were emptied into the woods and the little coffin was shoved into the garbage bag in her canoe. The awful smell of rotting worms wafted off the container and onto her fingers. She tried in vain to rinse her hands in the lake, but her fingers still reeked. Everything else looked set to go, except for the ladies; they looked visibly nervous. The wind was at its worst.

Michelle decided it was a good time to pray with the group and ask that mighty God of theirs for a little bit of His strength. When the prayer concluded, Michelle gave the ladies a quick crash course on how to deal with whitecaps.

"Before we get in our canoes and shove off, I'd better give you all a couple pointers. I don't mean to alarm you, but these whitecaps are dangerous. If your canoe is capsized, don't panic. Stay with the canoe, it will float. Your gear is all strapped in and shouldn't go anywhere. If you stay with the canoe, the wind will eventually push you to shore where the canoe can be emptied of gear and water. With your life jackets on, you should float and be OK. Now as far as paddling in this stuff, make sure the strongest paddler is in the back."

"DJ," Michelle said in her serious teasing way, "that's not you!"

All the ladies, including DJ laughed, momentarily relieving the stress of the life or death lesson. "Be very careful," Michelle continued, "not to parallel park with the whitecaps. These waves could catch you off balance and swamp your canoe before you even know it. Stay perpendicular to the waves. If you find yourself parallel parked, don't panic, keep your cool, and try hard to get perpendicular. I am going to try to crisscross behind some islands and that should give us a bit of a break. Other than that, just stay calm. Any questions?"

A nervous silence followed.

"OK then, let's shove off. The waves should push us straight to the boat landing. Try to have fun; this is a ride of a lifetime and you don't even have to pay to go on it."

The Alumacraft left the safety of the granite shore first, leading the way into the dangerous waters. The Grumman followed closely behind. A struggle immediately ensued. The waves wanted control and showed off their domineering power. With every ounce of strength, Michelle fought to keep the canoe perpendicular and moving in the right direction. The wind was playing cruel tricks on her. Without notice, it would shift directions opposite of the waves and push the Alumacraft parallel to the whitecaps. At their most vulnerable point, in the middle of a wide-open stretch of water, the wind whipped away the control from Michelle. She paddled as hard as she could but needed more power upfront to help move the canoe in the direction she wanted.

"Annie!" Michelle yelled. "Paddle harder! *Now!*"

Annie did not need to look back to see the expression on Michelle's face, she could tell by the terror in her voice that Michelle was afraid. Alarmed by the fear in Michelle's voice, Annie froze. She was unable to paddle, move, or even think.

Seeing Annie's immobility, Michelle grew silent with prayer and threw all her effort into another attempt to steer the craft. The wind shifted, helping to right the direction of the canoe. Seeing a point of land ahead, Michelle dared a glance back toward the other canoe. She could not see it. It was not there.

"Annie, we've got to get to that point and get on shore. I can't see the others." It was a difficult challenge to land the canoe without it getting battered against the rocks. They managed to get the canoe teetering upon a rock. Leaving Annie with the canoe, Michelle ran down the shoreline hoping to catch a glimpse of the Grumman. As each moment passed, the intensity of Michelle's panic grew. After what seemed like an eternity, Michelle saw the ladies paddling around a point. They had been unsuccessful in taking the same course as Michelle and were now catching up.

Running back to Annie, Michelle pushed their canoe into the water, and the two ladies headed around the point just ahead of the Grumman, aiming for the island. The canoes slipped into the shelter of the island's temporary windbreak. The momentary reprieve helped Michelle get reoriented before leaving the temporary safe haven. Another island lie directly ahead, and it was in that direction the canoes headed. This island was larger than the first, offering more of a buffer between the ladies and the rough water.

Michelle, seeing that the Grumman and its passengers were holding up just fine, turned her head from them to scan the distant shoreline. She saw what she thought was the boat landing and headed toward it. By the time she realized the opening in the shore was not the landing but rather the beach of a resort, it was too late to change course. To change direction to the real boat landing further on the left would have been disastrous. The ladies would be forced to paddle parallel to the whitecaps if she chose to change course. Not even Michelle had the courage to do that.

Michelle wanted to get mad at herself for making such a mistake; she should have studied the map more thoroughly. The group would have to land at the resort, and she would have to walk two miles to the landing to retrieve her truck. *No. This was God's will. He has a purpose in this mistake,* she thought. *I will just thank the Lord and push on.* The load on her mind was lifted. As long as she could keep the canoe moving in a straight line with the waves, they would be OK. Michelle relaxed and wished she had a sail with her. They were making excellent time. The ride was definitely an adrenaline rush.

"Have you ever had a ride like this before?" she asked Annie.

"Never."

"This would be really fun to do with an empty canoe and a good sail."

Annie wasn't so sure she agreed. She was just starting to pull herself together.

"Sorry I 'spazzed' out at ya earlier."

"Oh that's OK. Sorry I froze up on you."

"I noticed you were a little scared," Michelle said cautiously.

"That's only because I noticed you were a lot scared," retorted Annie.

With a chuckle in her voice, Michelle declared, "I think we're going to live." The two ladies enjoyed the rest of the ride. When the wind whipped hard, an occasional "hee haw" could be heard floating away in the mighty breeze. The heart-pumper of a ride ended as the canoe came to a gentle stop on the sandy beach of a resort. A man and woman sitting together on a wooden swing greeted the ladies. "Rough day to be out for a canoe ride."

"We didn't have much choice," Michelle said, visibly happy to be standing on solid ground.

"Looks like you just came out of the woods," the woman stated.

"Yes. We were out all weekend," Michelle politely replied.

"Good thing you came out when you did. The weatherman is warning everyone about the nasty storm coming this way. Should be here soon."

"I had a feeling this wind was bringing one," Michelle told the couple as they watched the Grumman glide onto the beach.

DJ hopped out of the canoe, exhaling a breath of relief. She felt like kissing the beach. Land never looked more beautiful to her, and never before had she prayed as hard as she did during that canoe ride. She burst out singing a song of praise to her Deliverer. Karen and Jenna were equally as thrilled to be on solid ground; they feared the ride would never end.

DJ's melodious voice tickled Michelle's ears, provoking a smile, yet leaving a little ache in her heart. She would miss hearing DJ's voice in the background. Within a day, Michelle knew she would be having withdrawals and would have to call DJ just to hear her voice. If Michelle needed a quick fix, she could always listen to her CD from their church play of *The Centurion*. DJ's solo was on track number one. Michelle chuckled as she remembered listening to DJ's song months ago with Shayla. Knowing that her mother sometimes missed hearing DJ's voice, Shayla said, "Mommy, you don't have to call DJ anymore, you can hear her voice whenever you want now."

Michelle shoved the ache in her heart aside and walked over to the ladies. "Is anybody up for a hike? My mistake will cost us about two miles of walking. It would be nice for at least one other person to go with me so we can drive back both vehicles."

"A little hike actually sounds like a good way to wind down. I'll go with you," volunteered Jenna.

"OK, but first let me go to the office and make sure they don't mind us being on their property. I'll explain what happened."

Michelle walked over to the office and waited inside for someone to come to the front desk.

"Hi, I'm Jon. How can I help you?"

"I just wanted to check in and see if it was OK to leave our canoes and gear by the beach while I walk to the boat landing. My group of women and I mistook your resort for the boat landing and were unable to correct our course in time."

With a smile of understanding Jon asked, "Would you like a ride?"

"That sure would beat walking. Thanks."

"I've got to go retrieve my keys. I'll meet you outside with the van."

Michelle went out and told Jenna the good news and the two ladies waited for Jon to pull up in the van. The ride was greatly appreciated. They thanked Jon, and Jenna slipped him a five-dollar bill and a Bible tract that shared the gospel. Michelle smiled at Jenna's thoughtfulness and quietly prayed, "Missing our boat landing wasn't a mistake, God. Please bless that tract and may Jon's heart be soft to receive it."

The ladies drove back, each in their own vehicle, and loaded up their gear. With everything set to go, hugs were exchanged, and a promise made to swap photographs at a later date. The trip was over. The ladies parted and Michelle drove home with a heart full of gratitude for her great God who worked out all the details of this wonderful experience. The memory of this special birthday trip would linger in her mind and warm her heart on cold winter days.

EPILOGUE

As Michelle stood at her kitchen sink, her idle hands rested in the warm sudsy water. As she gazed out the window at the snow-covered ground, a faraway look caught in her eyes. Jerry noticed the dreamy look that entranced his dishwasher. Wrapping his arms gently around Michelle's waist, he rested his chin on her head and asked, "Michelle, what's your wildest dream?"

The question brought her mind reeling back to the present and with a giggle she said, "You don't want to know."

"Seriously. What is your wildest dream?"

"It might not be wild enough for you, but it's to go on another camping trip with the ladies."

Turning his wife to look at her he said, "Why don't you go winter camping?"

"You can't be serious? I've never done that before."

With a straight face, Jerry offered, "I'll baby sit the kids for you."

"You are serious, aren't you?"

"Yes, I am. I dare you to go."

Michelle reached for the hand towel and wiped away the suds. She sat down on the wooden bench and rested her back against the log wall. Jerry smiled as he observed his wife so lost in thought.

"You'll really baby sit?"

"Yep," he said without a hint of joking.

Michelle stood up, studied Jerry's face, paused, and then headed for the phone. She looked at her list of phone numbers taped to the refrigerator and dialed. An adventurous voice answered with a perky "Hello."

"Hi, Stephanie. This is Michelle. Would you be interested…"

LaVergne, TN USA
25 May 2010
183811LV00001B/15/A